Bolan had stepped into a den of lions

There was a look of demonic rage, even desperation, in Zharkov's eyes. It warned Bolan the enemy was going to the mat to save whoever or whatever was inside that warehouse.

The Executioner peeled away from the relentless stammer of the AK-47 on his flank. He needed to make his move. He knew Grimaldi was outside, ready and waiting, itching to drop the hammer.

The way looked clear as Bolan headed out.

That changed in the next heartbeat when Zharkov rounded the corner, smiling as he opened fire.

MACK BOLAN ®
The Executioner

DON PENDLETON'S

THE EXECUTIONER®
RISK FACTOR

A GOLD EAGLE BOOK FROM

WORLDWIDE®

TORONTO • NEW YORK • LONDON
AMSTERDAM • PARIS • SYDNEY • HAMBURG
STOCKHOLM • ATHENS • TOKYO • MILAN
MADRID • WARSAW • BUDAPEST • AUCKLAND

First edition January 2000
ISBN 0-373-64253-9

Special thanks and acknowledgment to
Dan Schmidt for his contribution to this work.

RISK FACTOR

Opportunity makes a thief.

—Francis Bacon

The weapons of mass destruction are now used as a bargaining chip, opportunistically, at the expense of innocent lives. But I make no deals.

—Mack Bolan

THE
MACK BOLAN®
LEGEND

Nothing less than a war could have fashioned the destiny of the man called Mack Bolan. Bolan earned the Executioner title in the jungle hell of Vietnam.

But this soldier also wore another name—Sergeant Mercy. He was so tagged because of the compassion he showed to wounded comrades-in-arms and Vietnamese civilians.

Mack Bolan's second tour of duty ended prematurely when he was given emergency leave to return home and bury his family, victims of the Mob. Then he declared a one-man war against the Mafia.

He confronted the Families head-on from coast to coast, and soon a hope of victory began to appear. But Bolan had broken society's every rule. That same society started gunning for this elusive warrior—to no avail.

So Bolan was offered amnesty to work within the system against terrorism. This time, as an employee of Uncle Sam, Bolan became Colonel John Phoenix. With a command center at Stony Man Farm in Virginia, he and his new allies—Able Team and Phoenix Force—waged relentless war on a new adversary: the KGB.

But when his one true love, April Rose, died at the hands of the Soviet terror machine, Bolan severed all ties with Establishment authority.

Now, after a lengthy lone-wolf struggle and much soul-searching, the Executioner has agreed to enter an "arm's-length" alliance with his government once more, reserving the right to pursue personal missions in his Everlasting War.

1

In combat all men were not created equal. A combination of hard experience and lethal skills honed to deadly perfection on the battlefield usually provided the advantage needed to be the one left standing. Of course, when the bullets started flying all bets were off.

Mack Bolan was well schooled in this kill-or-be-killed reality, and had more than earned a warrior's claim to firsthand ownership of the edge. Right then his gut instinct tipped off the man also known as the Executioner that once again he would need to seize all the advantage he could get.

He knew he was being followed. They were nearly as obvious as the Manhattan skyline looming across the East River, and had been just as brazen in their tailing of him since they had pulled up behind him outside the terminal at La Guardia airport.

The big soldier tightened his grip on the steering wheel of the Jeep Cherokee as he threaded his way through the maze of traffic in New York's most populated borough, Queens. He was a few minutes off the Long Island Expressway, making his way north on Jackson Avenue and moving into the commercial heart of the neighborhood. Through his dark aviator sunglasses he scanned the fronts of butcher and jewelry ~~s,~~ the shingled homes, the small restaurants and cafés. Everything tight and cluttered, everyone hustling along, as the dark sky rumbled and threatened rain. The soldier was looking for a suitable alley, something long, with an adjacent exit. Something lonely.

His jaw was clenched, his heart beating faster with the anticipation of enemy contact. Even if it proved a false alarm—and he didn't think so—the Executioner had come to New York prepared for total war. Beneath his loose-fitting black windbreaker he toted his standard and proved hardware. The 9 mm Beretta 93-R was snug in the shoulder holster, while the .44 Magnum Desert Eagle rode on his hip. On the back seat a large canvas bag contained an Uzi submachine gun, an M-16 with an attached M-203 grenade launcher, plenty of spare clips and a mix of frag, incendiary and smoke, and flash-stun grenades, just in case the enemy numbers began increasing and Bolan needed to clear an area in a hurry. If the intel was correct, then the opposition was suspected of controlling an international ring of human mules smuggling nuclear materials on commercial flights. If so, Bolan feared full-scale battle could erupt in the Big Apple.

Especially if the Russian Mafia knew the FBI was on to them.

It looked, though, as if the soldier's game plan had suddenly changed, at least for the moment. Bolan needed to find out who was shadowing him and deal with any back-door threat before the main event got under way.

Up ahead he watched the black Lexus. Three known Palestinian terrorists were inside the vehicle, and they were part of the reason Bolan had come to New York. A simple snatch for some Q and A, though, felt destined to fall apart. The intel had stated that these i national terrorists might be couriers of U-235, U-238 and Pu-239, and possible component parts necessary to build a light-water reactor to process fissionable nuclear material.

At the moment it was pretty much guesswork and instinct on Bolan's part about the enemy's intention and operation. With countless questions nagging the soldier he had more than a few good reasons to believe this mission would start off going straight to hell.

Early that morning, before Bolan boarded a military flight for LaGuardia, Hal Brognola, the big Fed from the Justice Department who also oversaw and ran the covert operations at Stony Man Farm, had alerted him to the potential situation. It had been learned that Ali Fusein would be flying to New York with another Hezbollah fanatic on a nonstop flight from Moscow. More questions than answers kept tumbling around Stony Man Farm, and Bolan was sent out.

Which meant he'd do whatever was necessary to get the facts, uncover the enemy and terminate their operation. And the few facts at hand were weak and mind-boggling, but the Man from Justice along with his team at the Farm were uncovering more details by the hour.

The terrorists were in New York, Bolan suspected, to pick up something for delivery to an unknown destination. And if that was happening then there was a good reason why Ali Fusein looked deathly ill. Bolan had watched the fanatic sweat and convulse his way to the waiting Lexus at the airport, the supporting arm of his brother fanatic locked around him. There must be a lot of money involved.

Briefly, the soldier debated the situation, weighing the pros and cons of continuing his own tail while being followed himself. The FBI special task force that Brognola had used his clout to get Bolan aboard and in charge of was in northwest Queens, near the East River. Special Agent Brian Winfrey had a team staking out the targeted warehouse, and when Fusein arrived they would still be on site, ready to drop the net over the terrorists. In fact the FBI had been investigating and monitoring the movements of Fusein, in both Moscow and New York, for nearly a year. Perhaps either in the interest of interdepartmental cooperation, or simply because time was running out, it was also Winfrey who had loaned Bolan his sports utility vehicle to follow the terrorists from the airport.

Bolan looked in the rearview mirror as he turned west toward the East River, the Queensboro Bridge to Manhattan spanning the river in the distance. He let the Lexus go on. Behind, he saw the black four-door sedan, its occupants hidden behind tinted windows, still on his tail.

Certainly someone else had been awaiting the arrival of the terrorists. Bolan's tail was either to make sure the Lexus got to the warehouse unmolested, or the opposition had changed its own game plan and was looking to eliminate a liability. And Ali Fusein had indeed become dangerous with his inside knowledge of the enemy's operation. The terrorist was obviously dying from exposure to ionizing radiation, so he had nothing to lose. He was also wanted by the FBI, Interpol and half a dozen other law enforcement agencies around the world.

The soldier circled the block. Since spotting the tail on the expressway, he had radioed Winfrey. The FBI agent had assured Bolan he had dispatched no team as an escort, then proceeded to remind Special Agent

Mike Belasko of the Justice Department that his job was only to tail the terrorists to the warehouse and keep the FBI team updated. All available agents, Winfrey had informed Bolan, were on hand and waiting for Fusein to arrive at the warehouse.

The Executioner found the alley he was looking for and spotted the sedan locked on his tail. It stood to reason they knew they were made as a potential threat.

The alley was a long trash-littered strip cut between two brick buildings. It appeared deserted as Bolan scanned the windows and doors, finding only a car passing the opposite mouth of the alley. If enemy contact was going to be made it would be soon.

No time like the present, the soldier decided, unzipping his jacket as the sedan slid up behind him. He quickly grabbed the .44 Magnum Desert Eagle in case the windows were made of reinforced glass, and beat them out the door. The edge belonged to Bolan, and not a second too soon.

It was something in the way in which the doors opened that alerted the soldier to sudden danger. Two big men in black leather bomber jackets and dark shades, with long hair and heavily bristled faces, didn't strike Bolan as law enforcement types. And the muzzle of an AK-47 assault rifle springing up over the back passenger door confirmed Bolan's worst suspicions.

The Desert Eagle was up and thundering. Bolan's first round nailed the hardman with the assault rifle, taking out glass and driving the gunman to the floor of the alley, as a burst of wild autofire sprayed brick chips off to his side. The other gunner behind the front passenger door almost had Bolan lined up in the sights of his .44 Magnum revolver. Not missing a beat, the Executioner swung the Desert Eagle's aim, squeezed the trigger and obliterated the snarling features behind the massive revolver.

Even before Bolan's second victim hit the ground, the unseen driver of the sedan suddenly decided to use the vehicle as an armed battering ram.

A shaved head poked out the back passenger window, an AK-47 flaming and jumping around in the gunman's hands. But the vehicle's forward lurch threw off the first few 7.62 mm rounds, as a line of bullets marched across the back window of Bolan's Jeep. Glass shattered and bullets tattooed spiderweb cracks along the front windshield. Bolan hit a combat crouch beside the Cherokee and squeezed the trigger as fast as possible. Two .44 slugs tore out the throat of the gunman, nearly decapitating him.

Bolan kept tracking.

The sedan roared on a collision course meant to bulldoze Bolan to bloody pulp. On the backfly, the soldier directed relentless fire at the windshield, going for the unseen driver behind tinted glass. Three cannon peals from the Desert Eagle and the soldier blew in the windshield, glimpsed a figure fold over the steering wheel a heartbeat before the sedan clipped the back end of the Jeep. Metal rended and glass shattered. Bolan hit the ground and rolled ahead as the impact flung the back end of the Cherokee toward him. As the sedan whipped past, the soldier tracked the unmanned vehicle from a crouch by the back fender until it hammered into a trash bin. Garbage took to the air as the bin flipped on its side, and the sedan shuddered on.

The Executioner was up and moving, fanning the sedan with the hand cannon as it grated down the wall, metal on brick, sparks flying, until it finally rolled to a stop.

A quick search of the alley, then the open mouth at the opposite end, and Bolan found no prying eyes. But this was New York, after all. Big, mean and aggressive, where violence was all too commonplace and most citizens tended to look the other way. It was just that kind of apathy Bolan counted on to get him clear of the alley.

Inside the sedan the soldier found only dead bodies. He could venture a strong guess as to who they were, but it would keep until he could contact Brognola.

Moments later, the Executioner hopped into his damaged loaner, dropped it into drive and rolled on. If the enemy was aware they were targeted, they would be scared and desperate. Factor in the means, money and men, then top it off with all the fear and anger of a savage cornered animal, and it looked like the Russian Mafia was suddenly pulling out all the stops to send troops into the streets to gun down ally and foe alike.

It didn't take instinct or hard experience to warn Bolan that all-out war was set to explode on the streets of New York.

BOLAN DEMANDED a sit-rep as soon as he rolled into the surveillance room. What the Executioner received from Special Agent Winfrey instead was anger and indignation. Worse, Bolan sensed panic and confusion in the air.

"What the hell happened to you, Belasko?" Winfrey asked, using the alias Bolan had chosen for this assignment. "Where have you been? You were supposed to keep me updated but all you do is check in to see if I've got my own people riding your bumper from the airport. Hey, hotshot, our boys beat you here by almost ten minutes. You stop for coffee and doughnuts, or what? Not only that, I just had three goons pull up and walk inside that warehouse, two of them with AK-47s slung around their shoulders, bold as the devil himself. In short, this situation feels like it's set to blow up in our faces. That's your situation report.''

Bolan looked away from Winfrey's scowl. He agreed that some unexpected disaster was waiting for the home team. With his M-16 with the attached M-203 grenade launcher hung from his shoulder, the soldier strode toward the window. Earlier, Bolan had been to the surveillance room in the boardinghouse to get a feel for the situation, lay out a plan of attack with Winfrey. Since simple and straightforward always worked best in Bolan's experience, the plan was for Agent Belasko to lead the charge, the first one through the front door, while a full squad of FBI agents wielding automatic weapons went through the side and back doors. Everyone would be masked and lobbing in tear gas.

The stakeout team was three stories up, across the street from the targeted warehouse, which was a large brick affair, roughly a block east on the outer edges of an industrial park. Bolan knew Winfrey had a sniper team on the rooftop, with a squad of FBI agents a block north ready to storm the warehouse from the rear.

Near the front door of the warehouse the soldier spotted the black Lexus but also found a red Saturn parked behind the terrorists' vehicle. There appeared no activity on the surrounding streets. Most of the buildings on this block were either abandoned or had been bought out by real estate developers looking to renovate the area, the moneymen perhaps longing to return Queens to its early glory days of ferry rides to Manhattan.

"Dammit, Belasko. I have to tell you I don't like this cowboy crap the Justice Department has dumped on me. The FBI has had a six-month stakeout on this warehouse. Fusein and two other known terrorists have been surveilled from this room since they first showed. I, meaning me and the Bureau, don't know what they're doing there, and if you and your Justice Department pals know, you're not saying. Yeah, I read you loud and clear, Belasko. All that need-to-know business. What I know about is some undetermined connection to the Russian Mafia, and that these three Hezbollah beauties are wanted as international fugitives who seem to have access to more money, forged passports and visas than the CIA. Our people had them damn near bottled up in Moscow before your boss..."

Bolan tuned out Winfrey's outburst. He knew it was essentially the FBI's investigation and the bust should belong to them. The problem was the FBI and other law enforcement agencies had clear-cut parameters they had to work within when dealing with the bad guys. Bolan wasn't restricted to merely slapping the cuffs on the enemy and reading them their rights.

The soldier looked at the heavily lined, grizzled features of the veteran agent and asked, "You said three unknowns went into the warehouse?"

"More than likely Russian Mafia killers, since we identified a couple of visitors to this warehouse a month ago as being some of Brighton Beach's finest hired guns."

Brighton Beach, Bolan knew, was the New York home away from home to the Russian Mafia. But where Palestinian terrorists, nuclear material and the Russian Mafia linked up, Bolan was essentially in the dark.

From behind his telephoto lens, and sitting next to the camera that was hooked up to a video recorder, the agent Bolan knew as Williams said, "We're running the plates on the Saturn now. If the car's not stolen, then we can ID our three unknowns soon enough."

"You've never seen those three before?" Bolan asked. "Not a clue?"

Winfrey walked up beside Bolan. The soldier noticed the handheld radio clutched tight in his fist. Winfrey lifted a pair of field glasses to his eyes. "If I had I would have said so. The thing about the Russians, which makes them damn near impossible to infiltrate, is the cultural and language barrier, but that's just for starters. They are the most paranoid group I know, xenophobic to a fault, or a virtue, depending on how you look at it. They're as tough to crack, if not worse, than the Chinese Triads. And even within their own tight little community in Brighton Beach not even the good people will talk out against the Russian *mafiya*. Throw in the fact that stoolies and traitors meet a quick demise, plus the execution of said stoolies' entire families—and, if you can believe it, in an even gorier fashion than the Colombians dole out—and you've got fear spreading like a cancer. Everyone looks the other way, keeps their mouth shut. Now, try sticking an undercover op in Brighton Beach and you might as well put a neon sign on the guy's face. 'Hello, comrades, I'm FBI and I'm here to find out what the hell you're up to and have you and your Don arrested.' Not only that, when they hire muscle to take out someone they don't like or has stepped on the Don's thousand-dollar Italian imports, the hired guns are flown in from Russia, forged paperwork up the wazoo, do their wetwork and grab the next flight out of La Guardia for the motherland.''

Bolan knew all this from firsthand experience, but it seemed to bolster Winfrey's self-esteem to state the obvious and let the troops know he knew the score. Suddenly the front door of the warehouse opened, and the soldier's grim attention riveted on the action unfolding across the street.

Bolan found an extra pair of field glasses. He adjusted the focus and scrutinized the three unknown faces. The men were dressed in black leather bomber jackets. One had shoulder-length black hair, another had a face like an ax, and the third man was a giant with a crew cut white as snow. And, just as he had been informed, two of the unidentifieds had AK-47s slung from their shoulders. Ax Face and Crew Cut were carrying black canvas bags. Something, Bolan sensed, was happening too fast. Something in the way the unidentifieds moved, looked around, arrogant, in charge of the moment.

The radio crackled in Winfrey's hand. A voice that sounded urgent to Bolan said, "Bilton here, sir. I believe we just heard gunfire inside the target compound.''

"Those satchels are empty now," Williams said. "They weren't before. What the hell?''

Bolan looked over at the FBI agent surveying the street through his binoculars and saw the dark confusion etched on his face. Bolan's gut churned with bad instinct. The soldier heard Winfrey order Bilton, "Move in. Await my orders before you go through the door. What the... Look at the ballsy son of a bitch,'' Winfrey suddenly growled.

Larger than life in Bolan's field glasses, Crew Cut

was throwing the middle finger straight at the surveillance room and grinning as if he was dying to reveal some secret to his watchers.

"How the hell does that bastard know we're here?" Winfrey asked.

Good question, Bolan thought, then caught a glimpse of Crew Cut with a small black box in his hand as he piled into the car.

"Tell your team to fall back," Bolan shouted.

"What?"

The soldier snatched the handheld radio from Winfrey, patched through to Bilton. "Bilton, this is Belasko. I'm ordering you to fall back. It's a trap. Roger that, Bilton. Fall back now!"

Bolan heard the hesitation in Bilton's voice as he confirmed the order.

"Someone's stumbling out of the warehouse," Williams said. "It's Fusein. He's been shot."

Bolan saw the terrorist clutching his stomach. He'd apparently been shot low, either in haste or to make his suffering last longer, but Fusein appeared to be more concerned with moving away from the warehouse than holding in his guts.

Bolan heard the screech of rubber in the distance, glimpsed the Saturn disappear around the far corner.

"Hit the floor!" Bolan yelled.

2

A fleeting glimpse of a fireball expanding through the front wall and rooftop of the warehouse sent Bolan nosediving for the floor. The FBI agents were nearly a heartbeat too late in hitting the deck. They were tumbling for cover, shocked expressions etched on their faces, when their building took a terrible pounding from the tremendous ear-shattering explosion. The floor beneath Bolan shuddered.

The soldier covered his head as flying debris blew through the windows with meteoric force. Superheated wind and a deafening roar cycloned in behind the shattering glass and hurtled wreckage. Surveillance cameras, phone bank, fax, video recorders and the few pieces of furniture around them were crushed by the concussive force.

It seemed to go on for an eternity, as Bolan rode out the man-made storm, his brain feeling cleaved by the noise, debris winging off his body.

Ears ringing, feeling a warm stickiness trickling down the side of his face, Bolan checked himself quickly. Aside from a couple of scalp and facial cuts he was in one piece. He stood, squinting against the nearly blinding firelight beyond the gaping holes in the room, fisting the blood out of his eyes.

The soldier ran a gaze over the three FBI agents.

They looked up at Bolan with horror. "Everybody all right?"

From the sparking ruins of their surveillance equipment Williams and the other agent gave Bolan shaky nods. Winfrey cursed, stood on rubbery legs, wobbling like a drunk for several moments.

Bolan scooped up Winfrey's handheld, tried to patch through to Bilton. He had to call the agent's name several times before the Fed's voice cracked back at the soldier.

"Y-y-yeah, y-yes, sir... Goddamn...I...we were going to..."

"Check your men, Bilton."

While Bolan waited for a head count, he surveyed the street below. Everything smoked, burned, rained debris and crackled. The unknowns, he suspected, had used a whole lot of plastique explosive to inflict the kind of destruction Bolan saw. Worse, the blast might have touched off something far deadlier.

Radioactive waste.

Bilton came back on. "Sir, everyone is in one piece and accounted for."

"Bilton, clear the area. No one, I repeat no one, is to approach this street. That means you, your men, civilians and anybody else. NYPD will be en route as we speak, and they will receive their orders from Agent Winfrey. This entire blast area will have to be sealed off, and no one within a three-block radius—that's all points on the compass—is to come near what I'm designating as a no-entry zone. Get to the industrial park, secure that area likewise and round up any civilians you find and get them out of there. Copy that, Bilton."

"That's affirmative, sir."

"Stand by for further orders. Belasko out."

"What's going on, Belasko? What was in that warehouse?"

The soldier sucked in a deep breath. There were a few items he had purposely neglected to let the FBI in on. First, a team of blacksuits from Stony Man Farm had flown in behind Bolan. They had brought decontamination suits designed to protect them from exposure to radiation. In a few minutes they would be on the scene, suited up, tagged with Justice Department credentials, with sensors in hand to sweep the area for radioactive fallout from uranium dust, or any radioactive waste that might have been hurtled into the air by the blast. Of course, if that was the case, then Bolan and the FBI men were already exposed. Aside from being lethal at high doses, another problem with radiation was that it was unseen, without taste or smell, and could only be detected with sensors, or when a human fell deathly ill, and by then, it was too late.

Bolan hadn't told Winfrey about the possibility of exposure to radiation because he didn't want a general panic, for starters. It was also a mission without answers, no solid leads to put a face on the enemy. He didn't need SWAT, NYPD, the FBI, the CIA and the military with their own hazard team mucking up his play, everyone strangling him in red tape. What Bolan needed was to get in touch with Brognola, have the big Fed pull out all the stops and muscle the FBI to back off while giving him whatever intel they had. He had a good idea of who was behind this, but he needed names, a place to start.

Bolan scanned the street. Then he saw the figure, crawling beneath a pall of smoke and showering debris. Incredibly, Ali Fusein was still alive.

With his M-16 in hand, Bolan was out the door,

down the steps and on the street moments later. Feeling on his face the sear of roaring fire consuming the demolished warehouse, he scanned the devastation for any sign of life. Other than the dying terrorist, Bolan was alone.

He heard Fusein moan. As the soldier loomed over the terrorist he knew the Palestinian was seconds away from checking out. The terrorist's hands clutched the hole in his stomach.

"Fusein," Bolan growled. The terrorist looked up at the soldier through glazed eyes, then coughed blood. "You're not going to make it, Fusein. Your employers stuck it to you. They used you. They got what they wanted and cut you out. You want some payback, give me a name."

The terrorist choked on his blood, managed a short fit of laughter. "Ah, yes...payback...Russian bastards...Smol..."

"A name."

"Smolens...kov..."

Bolan heard footsteps behind him. He saw the light fade forever from the terrorist's eye. Turning, the soldier found Winfrey.

"I want this man choppered to the nearest hospital and cut open under your supervision. I need an autopsy report, ASAP."

Winfrey nodded. "Anything in particular you're looking for?"

"Uranium-coated pellets or pellets that contain U-238."

The FBI man's jaw went slack, and Bolan was treated to a new stare of horror.

A LITTLE MORE than three nerve-racking hours later, the Executioner listened to Hal Brognola's grim voice over the satellite link. The soldier had already updated the big Fed on his end.

"We may have a horror show on our hands, Striker. A problem, I'm afraid, of potentially apocalyptic proportions if our collective hunches here at the Farm are on target. It goes without saying we're working around the clock on this, and we've collected some more intel since you left for New York. Also we've run down the name you gave us, this Smolenskov. I'll get to that in a moment. The good news is our team didn't find any traces of radiation in or around the blocks surrounding that warehouse, and they were thorough, you can believe that. As far as exposure, you and the FBI team are safe. But our boy Fusein wasn't so lucky. He went under the knife, like you ordered, and I just received the report from Winfrey over at Bellevue. I'll let Kurtzman fill you in."

The soldier was alone in a safehouse in a middle-class Brooklyn neighborhood. Since Bolan was a frequent visitor to the Big Apple, the house had been bought by Brognola through the Justice Department budget, and it held everything the soldier would need when he dropped into the New York area. The small brick house sat alone at the end of the block, with every door and window hooked up to a central alarm system. Of course Bolan had the code and the keys to the place, along with the combination to the large vault that was built into the floor of the living room, beneath the carpet. If a burglar somehow did neutralize the alarm system a red light would go off at Stony Man Farm and the vault would be bathed in acid, melting everything from the blacksuit to weapons to satellite link into a puddle of goo. From the vault Bolan had taken the suitcase with its satellite link and fax, which he had set up at the kitchen table while he waited for Aaron Kurtzman's report over the Farm's speakerphone.

"The preliminary autopsy on Fusein," Kurtzman began, "indicates he died from high levels of exposure to ionizing radiation, probably from U-238 if the pattern holds, like the load that was confiscated by the FBI and Customs two months ago at JFK airport when that Russian collapsed on a flight to Moscow. Turns out the late Yevgeny Kliminska was former KGB, out of work since Russia supposedly went democratic and dismantled the KGB. We've nailed him as a soldier in the Family of the Boss of Bosses in Brighton Beach. Are you with me so far?"

"Uh-huh. Anything else on Fusein?" Bolan asked.

"Well, no pellets or cylinders of radioactive waste were found in his stomach."

Bolan knew time was critical, and he felt a growing sense of urgency. He knew where he was headed next but he needed a full report from the Farm.

"Now, exposure to radiation is measured in rems," Kurtzman continued. "Six hundred rems is considered lethal. Let me put it this way, Fusein was exposed to so many rems he might have glowed in the dark. Let me put it another way. Prolonged exposure to ionizing radiation and a man has a better chance of survival bleeding in the ocean in the middle of a shark feeding frenzy. This U-238 is created when U-235 is burned up in reactors. It's highly radioactive. You can get this stuff from any nuclear reactor. Hell, New Mexico's Homestake uranium mill has more than two-hundred million tons of uranium yellowcake piling up out in the desert. Couple that with all the nuclear power plants worldwide, the so-called dismantling of warheads in the former Russian republics, and the Russians have more than twenty thousand nuclear weapons stockpiled in more than one hundred storage depots. Money, means and determination will get a terrorist or any criminal cartel access to at least the basics to build a do-it-yourself bomb. At any rate, the obvious answer is that the seized radioactive waste is being transported to an end user, or skilled developer rather, who has access to a reactor. What happens is the plutonium is separated out of the waste and you've got Pu-239. Naturally you need the light-water reactor, the technicians and so on. We all know that terrorists everywhere have let it be known they're shopping for plutonium.''

"The obvious question then is where is this reactor.''

"Right,'' Kurtzman said. "Could be somewhere in Russia, although this stuff is being flown to Karachi and Somalia.''

"I'd rule out Somalia. I don't think they'll be a nuclear power anytime soon.''

"I'm not so sure, Striker, but I'll get to that. Anyway this atomic mule angle is something new in the world of black-market fissionable nuclear materials.

"It's usually moved by ship, not commercial flights. What's happening now is that the mules are risking exposing innocents, from baggage handlers to passengers flying all over the world, to radiation.''

"What's more, you can't get steel carbon containers through X ray at the airport,'' Bolan said. "Now we know about the ones who have died and the U-235, U-238 and even the plutonium that's been recovered has been found in the cargo holds of Aeroflot jumbo jets. We also know no one at Aeroflot, from the board of directors to the baggage handlers, are talking to the

FBI. What it tells us is that someone has the money and clout to pull this off."

"Enter the Russian Mafia. We both know the sorry state of affairs in the new and improved Russia. The Mafia owns that country."

Bolan knew that was sad but all too true. "And for the couriers dying off," he continued, "especially when two of them had advanced bone marrow cancer, it means this has been going on for some time."

"Even if they had been exposed to low levels of radiation over a period of time, meaning a hundred rems here, a hundred there, they would still get sick," Kurtzman said. "So you're right, this atomic muling has been going on for much longer than the past six months we know of. What I figure is that the couriers are more than likely being paid big bucks to handle nuclear materials that are questionably packaged. Say a warhead is supposedly dismantled in one of the former Russian republics, and the scrapped plutonium or uranium is being repackaged somehow. Or someone with clearance or who can bribe their way into a nuclear power plant has these mules ready to scoop up waste, shove it into a steel container, a seat-of-your-pants operation, then truck it off. What's even crazier is that they would ingest uranium pellets like the drug mules would coke or heroin. To do that they are either ignorant, desperate or suicidal."

"Or some timetable has been stepped up. And neither courier nor employer care about the risks," Bolan said. "Not to mention you need a whole lot of pellets just to make up one fuel rod."

Kurtzman sighed. "Exactly. Again it all points to the Russian Mafia. All the flights of dead couriers were traced back to Moscow or New York. All paid for in cash. Look, we all know there's a lot of scare talk around, usually in the media, about how terrorists can steal, say a small tactical warhead, a 100-pound 155 mm howitzer shell, point the gun and drop the shell on Tel Aviv or Washington, D.C., while having a smoke across the Potomac.''

"But only if they have the PALS."

"Right, without the supersecret permissive action links you've got a useless hunk of steel with some plutonium in it. And what terrorist has the capability of breaking into a half dozen or so U.S. military headquarters where you've got several million probable launch codes anyway, and a lockout system that shuts you down after three tries."

"So, obviously, they're looking to build something from scrap."

"Enough fissionable material, and your average fanatic has a neutron bomb with, say, a one-kiloton punch. Enough to annihilate everything within a 1500-meter radius. Not to mention, of course, radioactive fallout. Take out three blocks in any major U.S. city and the fanatic has made his statement. If he has six or seven of them you've got miniArmageddon or a hostaged city, ready to capitulate to whatever their demands."

"The Saudis in Somalia," Bolan said, recalling his earlier briefing. "What do you figure is the connection there?"

"That's where the line blurs even more. I ran a background check on the Saudis. They were close friends of a prince in the royal family, one Ali al-Aziz Kalbah. For the past two years, the prince has been in exile in Yemen. Seems he developed a heroin habit and the family kicked his butt out of the country before he

became a national scandal. Actually, it's not that unusual anymore. The oil-rich Arab nations have seen a
rise in drug addiction that's nearing epidemic Western-
type proportions. They're rich, they're bored, they have
too much time on their hands. Anyway, the Saudis used
to lop off the head of a drug addict or dealer, but now
every other family in the country seems to have at least
one member hooked on heroin.''

"The tip I received,'' Brognola interrupted, "from
a CIA operative in Yemen is that this disgraced prince
is very unhappy about being cut out of the family business, which, you can guess, controls a huge chunk of
oil, namely the Khawahr oil fields. Before he found
Allah through a needle, the prince would have inherited
more than eighty billion barrels of crude oil in those
fields. He's been seen in Yemen in the company of an
exiled Somali warlord, one General Akeem Assal. This
beauty, Assal, is wanted for war crimes and other atroc-
ities by Ethiopia and the government in the Sudan, not
to mention his own people want to string him up because of the man's ideas about population control.
Yemen, of course, is staunchly anti-West and has been
a main staging and training area for the exporting of
terrorists. During the Cold War Yemen was practically
owned by the KGB.''

"A lot of pieces, you're right, and none of them
fitting,'' Bolan said.

"There are more pieces to the puzzle, Striker,''
Kurtzman added. "The prince is known to have ties to
a faction of Hezbollah called the True Sons. As you
know, the Saudis are the guardians of Islam's holiest
shrines in Mecca and Medina. The True Sons are unhappy that sacred right belongs to the Saudis. They'd

like to see nothing more than the total obliteration of the two cities.''

More loose ends to digest, Bolan thought. But somewhere, somehow, there was a connection.

"What about Smolenskov?"

"That's your lead," Kurtzman said. "Colonel Vasily Smolenskov is former KGB. He landed in Brighton Beach ten years ago, and now owns a restaurant and several other businesses. Anyway, the owner of the warehouse that your unidentifieds blew up is listed as a jeweler in Brighton Beach. Both name and address of this jeweler are nonexistent. My guess would be Smolenskov. To further clue you in, the colonel was in the KGB with our Boss of Bosses, Yuri Drakovich, in Brighton Beach. The CIA also has a file on Smolenskov for some of his activities during the Afghanistan war. Seems the colonel had a talent for gassing the mujahideen resistance with nerve gas dropped from gunships. He's also suspected of opening his own opium pipeline during the war, using the funds to help create what has become the biggest and baddest of the Russian Mafia, which is located in Brighton Beach.''

"At least two and two are adding in that direction. Okay, send me all the files on every suspect from my shopping list. It looks like I've got my work cut out for me. And, Hal, since Able Team and Phoenix Force are on assignment I want Grimaldi," Bolan said, referring to his longtime friend and Stony Man's ace pilot.

"I'll get right on it," Brognola said. "We'll try and ID the three gunslingers who followed you from the airport, but it's probably like you said. They were Russian muscle flown in from the motherland with false paperwork. Watch your back, Striker. If the enemy is desperate enough already to send the guns onto the streets and start wasting any and everybody that makes them even twitch with suspicion…''

''I hear you.''

''You found the keys to your loaner?''

Brognola was referring to the black Cadillac, parked in the garage of the safehouse. The vehicle was armor-plated, with reinforced glass. Any tampering with the vehicle when Bolan left it unattended and the curious would get jolted with a nonlethal dose of high voltage, but would wake up wondering what planet he was on.

''I'm ready to roll on this end.''

''One more item. It took some doing, but the FBI director of operations in New York has granted you a twenty-four-hour window to do what you have to do. They had an ongoing surveillance in Brighton Beach of the Don you want. They've pulled out, and they're pledging complete cooperation. I think the head man in New York was expressing his gratitude for the fact that you saved the lives of his people.''

''Only grateful I made it in time. Twenty-four hours,'' Bolan repeated, as the fax machine began to spill out his shopping list.

3

Whenever it all seemed just like a stroll down easy street, Yuri Drakovich felt his radar for disaster kick in. He hadn't survived two decades of service as a KGB operative and assassin, followed up by another decade of bribing, extorting, strong-arming and killing, by taking anything for granted on his bloody climb to the top.

Unfortunately for the man who had become king of the so-called Russian *mafiya*, his two sons seemed to believe if it was too good to be true then take the blessing and run with it. Or, rather, eat, drink and party the night away. How tragically American they had become, Drakovich thought.

The Mob boss set down his phone with an attached scrambler and examined the faces of his sons, as troubling questions rolled through his mind. The report from his soldiers in the field was most disturbing. He needed to form a plan of attack with his sons, but he suspected a severe dressing-down was in order. Or perhaps they needed a display of one of his infamous explosions of rage to get their undivided attention.

Father and sons were seated at a long mahogany table in the banquet room of his restaurant. It was a spacious room, with a huge wall-to-wall mirrored bar, pool table, sunken Jacuzzi, all the gold and silver trim-

mings of the privileged and elite in Brighton Beach.
Beyond the double oak doors, Drakovich heard patrons
indulging themselves with his food and vodka in the
main dining room. The sounds of laughter and garbled
talk in their native tongue gave him a fleeting illusion
of comfort.

For long moments he stared at his sons. If they
weren't blood relations, Drakovich would have
rammed their faces into their plates, then shoved the
bottles of chilled vodka down their throats, shredded
their Armani jackets to pieces and strangled them with
whatever strips of expensive material was left. In the
past he had been known to do just that to a soldier who
had failed him. Indeed, some tyrannical display was
called for right then, something Stalinesque on the
menu. A dictator's special.

Drakovich ran a meaty hand over his bald pate, felt
the grooves of scars on his scalp where enemy bullets
had whispered past his big-boned face. He shook his
head. His boys were oblivious to his dark mood. He
felt his blood throb in his ears.

The elder son, Vladimir, was the soldier of the Family. Countless times in the past, in both Russia and
America, Vlad had killed for his father, and was,
Drakovich silently admitted to himself, his pride and
joy. One of the older son's duties was to personally
sweep the restaurant, and all their other businesses in
Brighton Beach, for bugs. During the past week alone,
Vlad had found three bugs, one left under the counter
of their jewelry shop on Brighton Beach Avenue, one
under a table in the main dining room, one under the
bar outside. It seemed a waiter had been infiltrated into
the restaurant by the FBI. That waiter was presently
more than just unemployed. That traitor, in fact, was

now incinerated ashes in an abandoned factory in Brooklyn.

Drakovich rested his stare on Gregor, who was two years younger than Vlad but just as good-looking and with a passion for pleasure that rivaled his older brother's indulgences. Gregor was the brains behind the Family business, but he had proved himself capable of maiming and killing in the past. He had been educated in Moscow, held a business and law degree. Now he juggled the numbers of several dozen different books, oversaw all monies and overseas accounts for the Drakovich Family. Both sons were dark-haired, lean as rails, and with the Ukranian blood of their long-since-dead mother, Anna, they were blessed with her fine chiseled features. Pain briefly stabbed Drakovich as he thought about his wife, who had died many years ago from complications of alcoholism. Endurance had been Anna's armor, but it had finally cracked under the weight of loneliness, he knew. All the years he had given more of himself to his country as a KGB killer than he had to her. Ah, but hardship was forever the way of the Russians.

The past was a howling ghost to Yuri Drakovich, but if a Russian learned anything at all about the past, he knew how to stop repeating the same mistakes.

Drakovich lifted his short, beefy frame, clenched his fists and his jaw, felt the blood pound in his head. As he stood his sons didn't even offer him a curious glance. They might as well have been pigs at a trough, he thought. Drakovich looked at the shaved-headed giant, Boris Zharkov, standing by the door, with the other two former Spetsnaz commandos he had flown in from Moscow to do what they had done that afternoon. Drakovich ambled past his sons as they shoved beef into their mouths.

"My sons," he said to Zharkov, and chuckled. "Look at them, Comrade, and feel blessed to be part of the American dream. The dream is money, and, of course, wine, women and song. If they aren't careful, Comrade, they may choke on the dream. See, they need all their protein and all the courage my vodka can give them so they can be sure to satisfy their whores later." That drew a look from his sons. Moving toward the bar, Drakovich went on, "They tell me red meat, coupled with just the right amount of vodka, works better than this American wonder drug, Viagra."

Zharkov chuckled, but Drakovich spotted fleeting disdain for the sons in the giant killer's black eyes.

"Ah, yes, the good life this country has given us. Indeed, it is America the beautiful." Drakovich stepped behind the bar, picked up a bottle of vodka. "You see, I have learned the hard way the problem with freedom is that it's often earned at the price of much bloodshed." Between bites, he saw Vlad look his way, and his son suddenly looked at his father with fear. Gregor also stopped eating and turned in his chair. They both knew this was going someplace, and they knew they weren't about to be patted on the back for their hearty appetites.

The father hefted the bottle. "The problem with freedom is that there comes a price tag called responsibility attached to it. A responsibility that demands constant loyalty to Family and comrades as well as diligence and discipline in all matters of business. The average wealthy American has no fear of tomorrow because his world is in order and there's no rival or enemy seeking to put a bullet in his brain. So he can fall asleep on his pillow with a bellyful of food and drink, with whispered promises of love to women other than his wife. But with us, it's different." His voice trembled as he clutched the bottle to his chest. "With us there's always some dog looking to take it all from us. And if we soften too much and blind ourselves to the price tag of our freedom our own whores will turn on us and slash our throats! Look at you!" Drakovich roared at his sons and they flinched, forks poised in midair as moments ago they mistakenly believed the moment of danger had passed. "A withered hag could gut you open like a hog before you could even beg for your lives!"

Drakovich hurled the bottle straight at Vlad's face. The elder son saw it coming, and had time to duck as it missiled over his head, shattering against the wall. No sooner did glass and vodka hit the carpet than the doors opened. Two soldiers burst in, reaching for 9 mm Makarov pistols inside their coats.

The Mob boss trembled with rage, while Zharkov lifted a huge restraining hand, shook his head at the soldiers. They retreated back out into the dining room, closing the doors behind them.

An animallike growl sounded from Drakovich's throat as he grabbed another bottle and threw it like a ninety-miles-per-hour fastball at the back of Gregor's head. The younger son dived to the floor as the glass bomb streaked over the table and detonated against the far wall.

Drakovich walked out from behind the bar. He nodded, smiled, smoothing down his shirtfront with both hands. "I'm at least relieved to see they still have their reflexes," he said to Zharkov, chuckling. He was the only one laughing.

Long moments of terrible silence filled the room. Gregor picked himself up off the floor and sat in his chair. He and his brother froze, looking as if they wished they could disappear.

Drakovich addressed Zharkov. "Go with my men to the warehouse. There you will find three mules who are to be escorted, unmolested, to the airport. These mules are clean, meaning they haven't fallen sick. You'll wait for Colonel Smolenskov to arrive with further instructions. You and the mules will be given new passports and identities to get you safely to Moscow. The appropriate Customs people have already been paid off, so you'll encounter no unnecessary delays. Comrade, you have fulfilled your duty, and I thank you. You'll receive the rest of your money when you arrive in Moscow. But you are on standby and will await further orders. Don't disappear into the nightlife of Moscow. I'll have future need of your services. Dismissed."

Zharkov nodded, and he and the former Spetsnaz men filed out of the room.

Drakovich scowled at his sons. "Accuse me of being paranoid, accuse me of becoming senile in my later years, but am I the only one in this room concerned of certain recent developments?"

Vlad cleared his throat and nervously said, "Father, with all due respect, I have warned you about the nuclear couriers, their exposure to dismantled warheads in the stockpiles, the handling of poorly packaged radioactive waste, leaking containers...."

"Indeed you have voiced your concerns. What's life without risk anyway? They knew the risks. They took obscene amounts of money from me for their services and they are fanatics to their own twisted cause. They have a death wish, this dying in the jihad, their holy war, but that has made them willingly accept their own death sentences. And it has furthered my own destiny, and put both of you in positions to inherit the kingdom with wealth beyond your wildest fantasies. Our goal is in sight. As we speak, I have three very rich potential buyers. And as you know, the items will go to the highest bidder. Anyone, however, who has become a liability in this operation has been disposed of, just like the Palestinians this afternoon. Need I remind you both that this operation has been going on since you were in the army, Vlad, shooting rebel peasant trash, and while you were busy chasing girls in college and law school,'' he told Gregor. ''Under the CIA's nose I managed, years ago, to smuggle in the necessary component parts to a country that now has the capability to process uranium and plutonium into nuclear warheads. I have purposely left out many details not because I felt you both incapable of understanding, but because the fewer people who know the less chance of exposure.''

''But the FBI are like lice crawling all over us,'' Vlad said. ''Both here and in Moscow.''

''Oh yes, the FBI. By the way, I'm told by your soldiers, Vlad, the FBI has suddenly mysteriously pulled all their surveillance teams out of Brighton Beach.'' He watched the confusion shadow his sons' faces. ''A most curious development, since they were ready to arrest the Palestinians. It becomes even more curious. I ordered Dmitri and his team to tail and dispose of anyone who followed the Palestinians from the airport, but they haven't been heard from. I investigated the matter while you were both shoveling caviar down your gullets and drinking my vodka.''

"Were they arrested?" Gregor asked.

"I dispatched a crew to retrace their route from the airport. They were found near the East River. Or, rather, my men saw what was left of them being scooped up and put into body bags. A policeman on my payroll informed me that they were gunned down. The kind of holes that were put in them and punched through reinforced glass weren't made by any standard federal weapon. My policeman has ruled out the FBI."

"Who then?" Vlad said, and Drakovich saw the first sign of life flare into his son's eyes since they had begun feasting. Vlad wanted revenge for the killing of his close friend Dmitri Keltsin. Finally he was reaching his sons.

"I intend to find out. I can see it never occurred to either of you we may have become targets. In a few moments, after we have discussed how we will proceed, I'll call Smolenskov and inform him of how I'm going to work both of you into a sudden change of plans."

The sons remained frozen to their chairs as the father walked up to the table. Yuri Drakovich smiled, then gestured at their food. "Go on, finish your meal. Only pray it isn't your last supper."

To say Brighton Beach was Brooklyn with a boardwalk and sea gulls would be almost accurate. To call the community of one-hundred-thousand plus Russian emigrants the home away from the motherland of the Russian Mafia would be entirely dead-on.

The Executioner stood, alone, near a bench on the boardwalk. The gulls flapped near his tall figure, the smell of salt filling his nose as the ocean lapped gently against the shore.

Night had fallen and the soldier was loaded for war, geared up and ready to go. While waiting for his one-man backup to arrive, the soldier had spent the past few hours poring over the intel on the Drakovich Family, forming a plan of attack.

It was a simple plan, but the soldier knew simple always worked best.

Feeling the weight of the Uzi submachine gun, slung around his shoulder and hanging down his side beneath the long black trench coat, he watched the shadow get closer. Bolan waited until the lean black-clad figure of Jack Grimaldi rolled up beside him. The soldier gave his friend and Stony Man's ace pilot a warm smile.

"The Farm briefed me, Sarge. It's a familiar enemy, but this bunch, I have a feeling, will be a little more savage once we put the heat to them."

"I've never underestimated the enemy."

"Ready to roll whenever you are. I take it you have a game plan for our friends in the Russian Mafia?"

Bolan nodded, his expression grim. "It seems our man Drakovich likes to play with fire. I learned that a lot of businesses here that used to belong to average Russians, who came in search of the American dream the honest way, have been torched. When the insurance companies investigated and wouldn't pay off because of clear indications of arson guess who stepped in and bought off the former owners and the property."

"The proverbial 'fight fire with fire,'" Grimaldi said.

"That will be our grand finale."

"I've always liked your style. Here's one of the items you asked for."

Bolan took the chronometer, which would also dou-

ble as a Geiger counter, from Grimaldi and attached it
around his wrist.

"We have less than twenty-four hours to burn down
Drakovich and get some answers along the way," Bolan said. "Here's the plan...."

4

The enemy would prove no easy pickings. But the Executioner was going in expecting nothing less than total and fierce opposition.

From brutal past experience Bolan knew that, beyond the lawyers and accountants, the bankers and smattering of legit businessmen who operated as fronts and patsies, the working body of the Russian Mafia consisted of former KGB operatives or ex-Spetsnaz commandos. Too many of those former military men and intelligence officers had found themselves unemployed, disillusioned and embittered about the new face of Russia, wondering what tomorrow would hold for them other than vodka and dwindling rubles. What Bolan would face were men with proved martial skills, the toughest of the tough, who had been looking for a way to get their lives back on track when the new Russia was born, for a chance to seize the fledgling capitalist dream no matter what it took. But the path they often chose on the way to rebuilding their lives—selling their souls to gangsters who tortured, maimed and snuffed out the guilty and the innocent alike without even blinking—would gain them no understanding or compassion from Bolan.

The Drakovich Family, as indicated in the Farm's intel, was no different. In fact, Yuri Drakovich didn't hire a man unless he had previous soldiering or killing experience.

With that in mind, Bolan found a dark alley and parked the Cadillac two blocks away from the house of his first hot suspect.

It was a quiet residential neighborhood, the rows of frame houses clustered tight, but separated by narrow alleys that seemed to go in all directions. The first of the soldier's stops was several blocks away from the frenzied nightlife along Brighton Beach Avenue.

Bolan got out of his vehicle, then hit the button on the small remote to activate the juice that would discourage theft. He had already done a drive-by on the target house. The way looked clear, but it wouldn't be unimpeded.

The FBI had been running surveillance on Vasily Smolenskov, had a file on the ex-KGB-operative-turned-jeweler that went back to his days as a mass murderer of innocents in Afghanistan, as well as covering his comings and goings in Brighton Beach. He was suspected of running a major fencing operation of hot gems, both in New York and abroad. If Smolenskov had a bag full of gems on hand, and if Bolan could seize a war chest the first time out, so much the better. The appearance of brazen robbery would further his cause. A psych-war jab might drive fear and confusion into the Mafia ranks, have them looking over their shoulders, stabbing fingers of blame and accusation at one another, and looking for enemies who weren't even in the picture while Bolan and Grimaldi tightened the noose. After all, Yuri Drakovich had bludgeoned, shot and brutalized his way to the top. The Don had plenty of enemies.

To further aid Bolan's play it also seemed Smolenskov stuck to a predictable routine. He would close up shop, same time every night, return to the home where he lived by himself, then contact a call girl waiting for a quickie. When he was finished playing, Smolenskov would ship her off in a cab. According to the FBI intel, the house was guarded by three armed soldiers. Those were the numbers Bolan hoped to face. If Smolenskov played to habit, the Executioner could be in and out with little fanfare. If all went according to plan, this would be round one to launch his keep-it-simple strategy that would get the Drakovich Family flushed out and scrambling right into the big bang.

Minutes ago, Bolan had found one soldier out front by a red Taurus, chain-smoking and looking as if he was killing time while waiting to take the boss somewhere. As if fate was helping to get any innocents out of the line of fire, Bolan had seen a leggy blonde hop into a cab when he drove past.

He checked his chronometer. Grimaldi would right then be making his own play near Brighton Beach Avenue. Timing, of course, would prove critical to success. Both Stony Man warriors had proven themselves, time and again, rolling the dice, coming up winners. Winning, the soldier knew, meant burning down the enemy, walking away in one piece.

The soldier rounded the corner, his combat juices flowing. He found the lone sentry lighting up another smoke. A quick check of the block and Bolan saw no one. Another look at the two-story house, and he spotted a light in the window of an upper bedroom. The front door at the top of the porch was ajar. No shadows fell over the opening right then. Bolan knew he would have to move quickly.

The Executioner reached inside his coat, closing on

the goal. He fisted the sound-suppressed Beretta 93-R, sliding it free of its holster. Ahead, the hardman drew deep on his cigarette, leaning against the front passenger side of the Taurus, oblivious to the moment. Bolan and sentry were all alone.

The Executioner was maybe thirty feet and closing on the hardman when the smoker looked up, spotted the extended muzzle of the Beretta.

True to plan, the Executioner kept it simple.

UNDER DIFFERENT circumstances, Vasily Smolenskov would have congratulated himself with a few vodkas, then bragged to the troops guarding his home that the old soldier still had it. A bellyful of meat, the just-right flow of vodka in his veins, and he had taken his pleasure from Helena of Norway—one of many call girls he rotated from Madame Zen's escort service in Brooklyn.

Alone in the bedroom now, the short, stocky, white-haired former KGB operative took a moment to feel pleased with himself. He wanted to believe he had even caught a satisfied twinkle in the call girl's eyes. Of course, the gleam could have resulted from the five hundred dollars and diamond ring he had given her before sending her off. No, he wasn't about to fool himself. Diamonds were a girl's—call girl or otherwise—best friend. At his age, the mind was always willing, but the body sometimes wasn't up to task. Tonight he had been a one-man Mongol horde on a rape-and-pillage spree.

Fear always motivated him to perform at the top of his game. Indeed, normally Smolenskov would have toasted himself. But tonight wasn't the night to let himself get too carried away. He could feel the operation slipping into some area of potential disaster. Already the timetable for delivery, production of the merchandise and the subsequent bidding war had been stepped up. Earlier, he would have sworn he smelled desperation on the Drakoviches.

As he closed the floor safe, slipped the rug back over it and stood by the bed he became grimly aware that the operation had been uncovered by the FBI. With the mules dying off aboard international flights, dropping dead in airport terminals, the FBI, the Justice Department, Customs, CIA and Interpol were suddenly alerted to the operation that had been going on for more than two years. Foolproof, he had thought, in that everyone who could endanger the operation had been paid off, or killed if they got cold feet.

But the unexpected always happened, and in order to survive the unforeseen a soldier had to adapt.

Smolenskov, Drakovich and sons were adapting. They were shifting every aspect of the operation back to Moscow—where it belonged anyway—where they were more protected by their own in the right power places.

The last of their mules were right now awaiting payment, along with orders to deliver merchandise from Moscow to a destination Smolenskov would receive only upon hitting the soil of the motherland.

He gazed into the silk pouch. The diamonds were flawless. Some were even up to forty carats. All in all, he thought as he cinched the drawstring, he had priced the load in the neighborhood of ten million dollars, American. Unfortunately one of the Pakistanis knew about Smolenskov's fencing operation and had demanded payment for his muling, half in cash, half in stones. It seemed Talik Mushad had a woman back in

Karachi he wanted to impress. It would be a pity to part with even a small handful of the stones, but Drakovich had given him his standing orders.

Gently he laid the pouch in his suitcase, next to the 9 mm Glock. He was shutting the suitcase, snapping the locks, when he heard what sounded like a scuffle from below, in the hallway.

A chugging sound was followed by a heavy thud. Alarmed, he darted for the window, thinking he was being raided. He checked the street. The FBI was everywhere these days, he knew.

Everything appeared normal—no armed, helmeted, dark-jacketed figures storming the premises. Except there was no sign of his driver, Pavel.

Smolenskov had moved back to the bed, was unlocking his suitcase when he spotted the big guy with the sound-suppressed gun roll through the bedroom doorway.

The Russian hesitated. There was something about the ice-blue eyes, about the way in which the invader held the weapon, that told the ex-KGB man two things. One, the intruder was no cop. Second and worse still, the big man was there with murder in his heart.

But Smolenskov wasn't about to go to the grave quietly. He threw open the suitcase, heard the intruder say, "You won't make it."

Smolenskov cursed, his hand sweeping for the Glock when the invader squeezed the trigger of his weapon, punching a hole through the suitcase. Smolenskov didn't flinch. He had the Glock in hand but discovered in the next eye blink that his reflexes were no match for the invader's lightning-fast surge. Smolenskov saw it coming, but he couldn't get his old body in gear to react. He felt the fist crack his jaw, saw the stars explode in his eyes and felt his body turn limp. The next thing Smolenskov knew he was on his back. Then, what seemed like hours later, he saw that grim visage looming over him. Smolenskov clung to consciousness, thinking the invader could just as easily have shot him. He was being spared, but why?

"Allow me to lighten your load."

The cobwebs cleared on that note, and horror and rage tore through Smolenskov as he saw his pouch being shoved into the coat pocket of the invader. Something, though, warned him this wasn't just a simple robbery. A second later, the invader confirmed it.

"Tell Yuri I know about the atomic muling. Tell him I'm closing his business."

An American, but who was he? Smolenskov thought. The big man took the Glock and backed toward the doorway. Smolenskov would remember that face and he would hunt the American down.

"It's only going to get uglier," the mystery man said before disappearing down the hall.

It took long and agonizing moments for Smolenskov to gather his senses. Somehow he managed to stand, even as nausea roiled in his stomach.

What the hell was going on? Slowly a terrible thought formed in his mind. Someone was coming after them, and they weren't looking to make an arrest.

No, Drakovich and associates were marked for extinction.

YURI DRAKOVICH had never known his longtime friend and business partner to sound so agitated. For a full two minutes, in between vicious bouts of cursing, Smolenskov had burned his ear about the mystery invader and the robbery of ten million in precious diamonds by a big American.

As soon as Smolenskov launched into his report, Drakovich had summoned Vlad into the banquet room along with a crew of twelve soldiers. The room now bristled with angry energy, Drakovich's dark gaze telling the troops there was trouble. Between bits and snatches of telling Smolenskov to calm down, he gave the orders for every man to begin arming themselves.

As Drakovich stood and moved to the bar, phone pressed to ear, he poured himself a vodka. The secret compartments in the far wall were opened and weapons were distributed among the troops. Clips were cracked home into assault rifles and machine pistols, while cylinders of Magnum revolvers were flicked open to check the loads.

On the other end of the scrambled line, he listened as Smolenskov continued his report. As usual they conversed in Russian.

"Comrade," Drakovich said, killing his vodka to get his own nerves under control, then firing up a cigarette. "You must remain calm. Start from the beginning," he said, and Smolenskov did. "You say he was an American?"

Drakovich listened as Smolenskov began. "*Da.* No mistaking. A big man, black coat and a silenced weapon that looked like a military-issue Beretta. This dark-haired American had the damnedest eyes I'd ever seen. No..." he corrected himself, "I know the look of a man who had seen and dispensed much death in his day. This was no policeman."

Very well, a non-Russian in Brighton Beach should be easy enough to track down. Drakovich would get right on it.

"You say he took the diamonds?" Drakovich asked.

"Yes," Smolenskov angrily replied. "But I have the other half of the pay...."

Drakovich felt his jaw tighten at the hesitation on the other end. He was already prepared for more bad news. "What? What is it?"

Smolenskov cursed. "I left it in the car with my driver. I'm moving downstairs now." More cursing. "My bodyguards are dead. Head shots. They never knew what hit them. Whoever he is he knows what he's doing. I'm moving outside," Smolenskov reported, as if he was right then peeking out the door, anticipating the shooter to pop out of the bushes.

Drakovich waited, and gave the entire situation some brief and dark thought.

He had known Smolenskov for a quarter of a century. Plenty of time to find out just what a man was made of, uncover flaws, faults, anything that might indicate if a supposed friend was motivated by hidden agendas. In the KGB, though, there were no secrets, and a man's character—or lack of—was always found out. If nothing else, Drakovich believed Smolenskov was a loyal comrade and business partner. They had killed together for the KGB, not only in Afghanistan, but on at least three different continents. Then, together, they had made the climb up the pecking order of the *mafiya* by systematically eliminating the competition, maneuvering all the right power people to make certain the Drakovich Family thrived and prospered. Was his dear comrade making a power play of his own right then? Was Smolenskov lying about the jewels, the robbery a hoax? But why? They had both planned this operation from its genesis, were the architects of a deal that would perhaps leave them the richest men in all of Russia. Given what had already happened to the crew found near the river, coupled with Smolenskov's encounter, there were too many questions and riddles flying all over the place. Drakovich would get answers, though, and they would only come with brutal, decisive action. Clearly it was a time to strike back.

Another disturbing question hit Drakovich. Smolenskov had been spared by their mystery American. Again, why? If Smolenskov was being one hundred percent honest in his report then the answer was obvious. The mystery shooter was using Smolenskov as human bait to get to bigger fish.

On the other end, Drakovich heard heavy doors open and close, then a string of vicious curses ripped over the line. "He killed them all! He took the cash, also! How am I to pay our mules now!"

"Calm down, comrade."

"I need a drink. I need to think."

"Stay where you are. I'll dispatch a crew to pick you up and escort you to the warehouse. I'll also send along the necessary funds. As for the Pakistani's payment in diamonds, you tell him we'll see to it at a future date. If he squabbles, if he gives you any crap at all, shoot one of his friends on the spot. Are we clear on this?"

"*Da,*" Smolenskov answered. "This couldn't be CIA, could it?"

No, he had never known the CIA to act so boldly on their operations. The CIA played shadow games, danced their operatives around Moscow through the American embassy. But Drakovich had too many eyes and ears in the right places, to warn him in advance about such dramatic tactics against him. He told his comrade as much.

"You don't think this is the work of one of our own?"

Drakovich knew what Smolenskov referred to. Over the years, in Russia and America, they had survived three shooting wars. The major group in Brighton Beach had been the Varsilikov Family. The Varsilikov clan was now dead, and what few soldiers had survived had been integrated into his own organization.

"No," Drakovich answered. "Our own wouldn't hire an American. Our rivals are either dead or on our payroll. Get back in the house and wait. I'll call you in exactly thirty minutes with instructions."

Drakovich dropped the phone, looked at Vlad who was wielding an AK-47, then addressed the troops. "It seems our problems are mounting. There is much mystery on the streets, and I don't like it. Comrades, let me explain what it is you are to do."

THE JOB ATE UP all of four minutes from start to finish. But Jack Grimaldi was on the clock, and he needed to check in with Bolan at one of three designated times they had agreed on.

Keeping to the darkest shadows of the alley, he moved toward the chain-link fence and tossed the empty canvas pouch aside. From some distant point he heard the laughter and sounds of music along Brighton Beach Avenue as people drank and danced the night away.

His first task was simple but dangerous, requiring stealth and swiftness, and keeping himself invisible from roving eyes. And the fireworks wouldn't even begin until the crowds thinned out and headed home.

At the moment, something felt wrong to Grimaldi. He felt an itch between his shoulder blades, one that could only be scratched when he made contact with an enemy he was sure was stalking him. Call it healthy paranoia born from instinct honed in the killing fields, but he knew Bolan would have finished round one by now. If it went down according to scheme—and Grimaldi didn't doubt his friend could pull off even the seemingly impossible—the enemy would be on high alert.

Meaning the hard force would hit the streets, shooting first, hold the questions.

Grimaldi took his own Beretta 93-R from its shoulder holster, attached the sound-suppressor before dropping it in the deep pocket of his long coat. He left his hand wrapped around the weapon, flicking the selector switch for 3-shot mode. On a shoulder sling, a mini-Uzi with a sound-suppressor hung by his side, just in case.

The Stony Man pilot gave the alley behind him a hard search. It was deserted. He had used wire cutters to make quick work of the fence Smolenskov and Drakovich used to keep drunks, intruders and anybody else from wandering onto the property. They had built a high privacy wall across the alley, topped off with razor wire. It was unlikely anyone would dare stray into the alley, out of pure fear of Drakovich and associates.

Grimaldi wasn't just anyone. In a few hours he would prove it with a flick of a switch and a thumb on the button.

The buildings Drakovich and Smolenskov had erected from the ashes of former owners were going to topple. The detonators on all five charges were tied into one radio frequency Grimaldi would detonate after he did a drive-by later to make sure the area was clear of civilians. Hermann ''Gadgets'' Schwarz had given him complete instructions before Grimaldi left Stony Man Farm. Enough C-4 was packed on the doors and staggered at intervals along the bases of the buildings to punch gaping holes, destroy the interiors and leave the owners with a headache and a lot of questions.

As Grimaldi squeezed through the hole in the fence, he gave the street another hard search, then laid the piece of fence he had cut back up against the hole. He didn't think any soldier of the Family would pop by and give the fence a close inspection but he knew anything was possible.

His rental was parked in a nearby alley. He was moving off onto a side street when he spotted a tall shadow break across Brighton Beach Avenue.

The shadow was heading his way, reaching inside his black leather jacket.

Grimaldi was made. He was rounding the corner of the alley, gripping the Beretta, when the sky seemed to drop on his face. Grimaldi hit the ground on his back, a fractured white light in his eyes. Someone had drilled him, and good. Desperation, fear and adrenaline kept the Stony Man pilot from going under. The only hope was that the opposition was, indeed, looking to ask questions first. Through the ringing in his ears, he heard a voice bark something in Russian.

''Who are you? Talk!''

A kick to the ribs, and Grimaldi heard his own sharp grunt, felt the nausea bubble in his gut. He looked up at the dark scowling face and saw the little machine pistol in the hardman's fist, aimed at his face.

Suddenly the hardman glanced away from Grimaldi

to yell something at his partner, the machine pistol wavering off track long enough for the Stony Man pilot to cut loose a 3-burst from his Beretta. It was quick, bloody but far from over, Grimaldi knew.

Holes exploded in the coat's pocket as Grimaldi's triburst ripped into the hardman's chest, dead center. How many were on his rear, Grimaldi didn't know.

Grimaldi rolled away as a short burst from the machine pistol was touched off by dying reflexes. The hardman toppled, the line of bullets hitting the pavement where Grimaldi's head was a heartbeat ago. Leaping to his feet, the pilot was greeted by the sound of thunder. A huge piece of brick was gouged out above his head, but Grimaldi was already tracking. The Beretta was out, and he squeezed off two 3-round stutters that nailed the goon on his rear.

Grimaldi shook his head, sucked in a deep breath to clear the fog and checked his surroundings. The alley ahead looked clear. The Stony Man pilot didn't hang around to congratulate himself. If there were two in the neighborhood, there would be more.

He broke cover at the end of the alley and moved as casually as possible when crossing Brighton Beach Avenue. It was then he heard the subway rumbling away. He hoped the racket the train made had covered the gunshots in the alley, but he was leaving nothing to chance. It was time to evacuate.

It seemed to take forever, his ears still ringing from the blow to the jaw, but Grimaldi willed the rubber out of his limbs and made it back to his rental car with no further enemy contact.

He spat blood out of his mouth. Pain then brought him crashing to a new and hard reality. If nothing else, the lethal encounter signaled Grimaldi the enemy had been shaken up on Bolan's end. From there on, they both knew the hunter could become the hunted.

But that was part of the plan. Hit and run, flush them out, crush them underfoot.

Simple but far from easy.

5

Bolan was wondering why Grimaldi was late for his call-in when the pager vibrated on his hip. Their plan was to silently page each other, just in case one of them was engaged with the enemy or couldn't find private space to talk on the handheld radios.

Roughly fifteen minutes had passed since the soldier's visit to Smolenskov. He had been tempted to page Grimaldi, but had waited, figuring no news was good news. Bolan had been riding out the time, driving around the neighborhoods, eyes peeled for a tail, then circling back to see who might have arrived to take a look at the Executioner's ideas on home invasion. It was a safe bet Smolenskov had run to the phone, alerting the boss to his unexpected troubles as soon as the intruder was out the door. Drakovich, he hoped, would gather the troops, a good piece of the enemy numbers adding up as they swarmed Smolenskov's residence, into Bolan's gun sights. Of course, all-out battle in a quiet slice of Brighton Beach wasn't on the table. With the suitcase, gun and a pouch full of diamonds, the soldier suspected Smolenskov had been en route for some sort of business coup. If that was the case, then Bolan decided to change the game plan midstrike, see where Smolenskov was headed.

The soldier picked up the handheld radio and listened as Grimaldi's voice came through. But Bolan detected something wrong in his friend's tone.

"Wolf Runner to Steel Talon, come in, Steel Talon."

Three blocks south of the target house Bolan eased the Cadillac down an alley, but stopped as he caught the sudden flurry of activity up the street. Three luxury vehicles were braking hard in front of Smolenskov's house. Doors were flung open and Bolan counted a dozen hardmen pouring from the vehicles. They were heavily armed and an air of angry energy swirled around the hard force. The cavalry had arrived, too late. If the hardmen weren't worried about the neighbors seeing all the AK-47s in full view, then it told Bolan that the neighborhood knew who and what Smolenskov was, didn't care or was intimidated into silence by the presence of the Russian Mafia living among them.

"Steel Talon here. What's your status, Wolf Runner?" Bolan asked, listening but watching as he spotted a familiar face popping into view when Smolenskov rolled down the sidewalk to meet the reinforcements.

Clearly the ex-KGB man was agitated. The colonel was gesturing all over the place, toward the Taurus and his house. A bald giant Bolan recognized as Drakovich's favourite assassin, Boris Zharkov, peered into the Taurus while a trio of soldiers bounded up the steps and went inside to check out Smolenskov's version of events. Then Bolan recognized the handsome face of the youngest Drakovich son from the intel pack the Farm had faxed him. As Bolan watched, Gregor Drakovich emerged from a Lexus, appeared to snarl something at Smolenskov, then tossed a duffel bag at the ex-KGB man, who caught it against his chest.

"Trick or treat was delivered," Grimaldi reported

on the radio. "But I was made. Enemy contact, engagement successful with minor dings and scratches to yours truly. I'm clear of the area and headed for strike point B. Two bad guys gone to the big vodka bottle in the sky."

Okay, they were made, Bolan thought. A glitch, no doubt, but the soldier had factored in a rapid response from the opposition. Enemy soldiers had obviously taken to the streets, Drakovich had been alerted and wanted to strike back, to find out who or what was responsible for his present crisis. Bolan could be sure Smolenskov had given Drakovich a full report, including a description of the American shooter.

"If I sound a little shaky on my end, Sarge, I got coldcocked on my evac. One of our dear departed landed a beaut on my jaw."

"You're alive and kicking, that's all that counts," Bolan said.

The hard force, Bolan saw, was suddenly piling back into the vehicles. A lone soldier took the wheel of the Taurus as the Drakovich son barked orders all around. There was no kid glove handling of Smolenskov as Zharkov hauled him to one of the luxury vehicles by the arm, depositing the jewel thief in the front seat. Engines roared and the minicaravan wheeled around, one by one, began peeling away in the direction opposite Bolan's position.

"There's been a change in the play," Bolan told Grimaldi. "Get out your map and find strike point C," the soldier said, the numbers tumbling in his head. Instinct told him something new was in the works. He was looking at his own map of the area, working on a hunch that the hard force was headed to a nearby warehouse Drakovich and sons owned. The FBI's surveillance had pretty much nailed the warehouse as a storage and transshipment site for narcotics shipped in from Colombia. The warehouse fronted as a trucking company that moved industrial machinery nationwide. It was easy enough to hide drugs inside machine parts. But Bolan wanted to believe he might find more at the warehouse than just dope.

"Before we initiate round two, Wolf Runner, I just want to mention I'd like to take a live one, if possible, this time out."

VASILY SMOLENSKOV felt like a leper, and he could honestly say he didn't much care for the feeling. He gave his predicament some thought, wishing to hell he had a scapegoat for his mounting anger.

A good ten minutes ago, Gregor Drakovich had whisked Zharkov and two other soldiers into the office of the warehouse. The younger son had actually scowled at the colonel, then dropped the blinds. The angry—no, the suspicious glowering the youngest son had laid on him since hauling him away from his home didn't escape him. This little lawyer pissant, he seethed, was wondering about his father's longtime friend and business partner's sudden woes, as if perhaps the whole damn thing was planned, some scheme he had designed to rip off the Family. Of course, Smolenskov couldn't be sure what the lawyer was thinking but he knew they weren't warm and fuzzy thoughts. Hell, the kid hadn't said two words to him during the short drive to the warehouse. And silence was far from golden right then. The looks, the scowls, the silent treatment were fraying Smolenskov's nerves even more. If Yuri Drakovich even suspected his business partner of making some Machiavellian power play then Smolenskov knew he was as good as dead.

The colonel fired up a cigarette. He looked around the large warehouse, as if expecting new trouble to come flying at them from all directions. Near the steel containers, beneath the ceiling crane, he saw the dark scowl on Talik Mushad's bearded face.

The three Pakistani mules had already voiced their unhappiness about the current state of affairs. They had been informed by Gregor about Smolenskov's misfortune and how they had to wait because Gregor needed Zharkov at the colonel's house. After the long delay cash delivery, courtesy of the young lawyer had been dumped into Mushad's lap, with a promise from the youngest Drakovich to finish the other half of the agreed-upon payment in diamonds once they were safely in Moscow.

"This isn't good, Comrade," Mushad suddenly said, his angry voice rumbling through the huge warehouse, jolting Smolenskov. "You're beginning to impress me as a man of many promises. Broken ones, I might add. We have gone to great risk for you people. I have even found out we've been exposing ourselves to radiation by muling for you."

The Russian gave them a mental middle finger. Nearby he spotted a half-empty bottle of vodka on a table littered with tools. He was stressed, tired, worried and angry. Under the watchful eyes of the half dozen soldiers near him, Smolenskov decided a drink was in order. He couldn't care less about the Pakistanis, or their Colonel Atta Tuhbat. The Pakistanis had been given a free ride into the country, money already put in their pockets and bank accounts back home, free room and board in Brighton Beach, including late-night visits by prostitutes, for a solid week. So what if the last part of the week had been spent in the warehouse under the guard of three soldiers in the Family carrying machine guns.

It all felt wrong to Smolenskov, and he experienced a sudden and deep stab of fear and paranoia. The mystery invader was out there somewhere, maybe had a small army to back him up. He had seen the face of death in his house, had been spared for a reason, and he suspected the American was using him as a human pawn on his personal chessboard. Forget the fact that another six guns were outside the warehouse watching the night, armed with AK-47s, and had even more powerful hardware at their disposal. Forget the fact that his vehicle and another car were parked near the closed doors inside the warehouse, ready for quick escape if something unforeseen happened. He was still nervous.

"Are you hearing me? This is going to make for a very long and unpleasant night, Comrade Smolenskov."

The colonel took a deep swig of vodka, had an impulse to walk right up to the guy and shoot him in the face, but simply told the Pakistani, "It has already been a long and unpleasant night."

"Things could get worse."

"Indeed. If that's meant to be some sort of threat, I would watch my tongue, if I were you."

"You aren't me, Comrade. We have different agendas. And my agenda demands money—and diamonds."

"I'm certain your whore back home can wait for her wedding ring."

The Pakistani's eyes lit with hatred. "If that's an attempt at humor, I don't find it funny."

"You see me laughing?"

Smolenskov stared down the Pakistani until Mushad broke eye contact and went back to counting his cash.

Gregor Drakovich, Smolenskov then saw, was walking his way, throwing dirty looks from the Pakistanis to Smolenskov and back. This boy, he determined, would never be up to facing what he had seen in the eyes of the American shooter.

The lawyer squared his shoulders. "There's to be no more talk about who has done what, who doesn't have what. We have urgent business to get on with. You are to act like professionals and honor your commitments. I hope I'm clear on this. If not, for someone, it won't only be a long night, but his last."

One of the soldiers began handing out the phony passports to the Pakistanis. As a "legit businessman" Smolenskov knew his paperwork was already in order.

Suddenly, at least half of the wall exploded in a ball of fire, screaming straight for his head. Smolenskov was hitting the deck as wreckage blew through the warehouse, when he glimpsed a familiar figure suddenly come blazing through a doorway. The American was now armed with more than just a handgun.

THE EXECUTIONER fully and grimly intended to spread the misery and misfortune around.

After linking up with Grimaldi at the rendezvous site following his brief tail of the hard force, the Stony Man warriors had ridden on and found a suitable dark alley to dump their vehicles. Even though he let the hard force drive out of sight, Bolan played to his hunch, checked his map, mentally marking off the way to the suspected target. Together they had moved in on foot, and found the warehouse guarded by AK-47 wielding shadows. Bingo. A deal was going down.

A quick but thorough recon of the vicinity and Bolan formed a keep-it-simple attack plan. They had been maybe five minutes late in arriving on site. Something was, indeed, going down inside the warehouse, some business dealing that must have been long in the works, Bolan knew. It was time to rain on the parade—with bullets.

Two vehicles had been left outside the closed rolling doors on the west side of the two-story brick building, along with six gunmen. He knew he could be facing a lot more guns inside. Either way, the soldier was carrying in the necessary firepower. Bolan had shed the trench coat for better mobility and shrugged on combat harness fitted with grenades.

After ironing out the small details, M-16 with attached M-203 grenade launcher slung around his shoulder, frag and incendiary grenades fixed to his combat harness and sidearms in place, Bolan had moved out. Grimaldi had made his climb up a fire escape to the rooftop of an abandoned factory just north and across the alley from the gathered hard force. Circling the perimeter to the south, the soldier had eaten up a few precious minutes getting into position, making quick work of the chain-link fence to the east with wire cutters, slipping through, then attaching enough C-4 to blow open the back rolling door.

Bolan knew Grimaldi was in position by now, above the enemy, with his finger curled on the trigger of his M-16/M-203 grenade launcher. If it went according to plan, Bolan would flush them out into Grimaldi's waiting gun sights. Of course, when the pilot heard the opening sounds of battle erupting, he would get busy with his rifle, dropping as many sentries outside as possible.

The Executioner placed a shaped charge of plastique the size of a quarter on the knob of the steel door, thirty meters up from where the big bang would happen, then moved and crouched behind a Dumpster. Remote in hand, Bolan hit the button and rode out the twin blasts. No sooner did the much smaller of the two explosions open the way for him, blasting the steel door inward, than Bolan was charging into the smoking maw.

The Executioner knew the enemy inside would look in the direction of the first and larger of the detonations.

As he cleared the smoke, he found they had, and the distraction gave him a heartbeat's edge.

Right away, Bolan went to grim work, M-16 blazing, set for full-auto slaughter.

They were picking themselves up off the concrete floor from beyond a line of wooden crates and steel containers. Of course the soldier had gone in not knowing exact enemy numbers, the layout of the warehouse.

There was cursing and screaming beyond the crates. Through the smoke and raining debris he spotted two shadows with assault rifles. The duo was spinning in his direction when Bolan chopped them off their feet with a short raking burst of M-16 autofire, flinging them to the ground, drenched in blood.

Engines gunned to life. From his point of entry the soldier couldn't see the vehicles beyond the crates and containers.

He was forging ahead when suddenly the giant with the shaved head burst around the corner of a steel container, spotted Bolan and held back on the trigger of his AK-47. Zharkov was either good, or psychic to have found him so quickly.

The Executioner was chased to cover behind a steel container. As 7.62 mm rounds whined off concrete and steel behind him, the soldier knew he had to make a move to outflank his enemies, or get pinned and shot to ribbons.

It hit Bolan then that he had stepped into a den of lions who weren't going to die quietly. Before falling to cover he'd glimpsed a look of demonic rage, even desperation, in the eyes of Zharkov. His was a face that warned Bolan the enemy was going to the mat to save whoever or whatever was in that warehouse.

The Executioner peeled away from the relentless stammer of autofire on his flank to make his move. He knew Grimaldi was outside, ready and waiting, itching to drop the hammer.

The way ahead looked clear, as Bolan darted down the side of the steel containers.

That changed in the next heartbeat, as Bolan saw Zharkov with his AK-47 wheel around the corner ahead, and cut loose with autofire.

6

Rolling thunder to the east trumpeted the call to battle for Grimaldi. Without hesitation, the Stony Man pilot got down to grim business.

From his rooftop vantage, he began laying waste the enemy, but quickly found out it wasn't going to be a turkey shoot.

Crouched behind the low retaining wall of the factory's roof, directly across from the gathered hard force, Grimaldi curled his finger around the M-16's trigger, the selector switch set for full-auto. He held back on the trigger, nailed one hardman by the Taurus, sent him flying over the hood, skidding out of sight. The enemy was vaguely outlined in the outer limits of hanging lights on both sides of the closed rolling door, mere shadows, but enough for Grimaldi's purposes. But as soon as their comrade went down Grimaldi found he was faced with stone-cold professionals who reacted without flinching to counterattack.

With AK-47s and AKMs clutched in their hands, the enemy was fanning the factory. No one was shouting or cursing down there. Instead, they broke away from one another, going for cover behind the vehicles or near a Dumpster, obviously knowing that to bunch up made them easy pickings. One of the hardmen even had the presence of mind to blow out the lights with two quick bursts of autofire. As darkness dropped over the alley, Grimaldi lost sight of the enemy.

It was time to throw some serious heat down there, the Stony Man pilot decided.

Grimaldi lined up his sights on the dark bulk of the Taurus, the breech of his M-203 grenade launcher filled with a 40 mm grenade. He released the hell bomb, watched as it streaked away and slammed into the side of the Taurus. A fireball erupted, shredding the vehicle, blowing a mangled stick figure into the side of the warehouse. The fire gave Grimaldi the necessary light to start tracking other targets.

He saw the rolling door coming up, then heard the sounds of autofire, cursing and screaming from inside the warehouse, engines gunning to life. When they rolled for evac, he would be ready.

Holding back on the trigger, he found it quickly became spray and pray with the M-16 as return fire began pounding the wall of the factory roof. Seasoned pros, they had marked his position, judged quickly and accurately from where his opening salvo was fired, and they were pouring it back.

Grimaldi glimpsed a shadow opening the trunk of the luxury vehicle, hauling out what looked like a rocket launcher. The shape of the warhead swinging his way told him the enemy was armed with an RPG-7 rocket launcher. They kept directing a relentless storm of lead, chasing Grimaldi to cover, stone chips flaying his face.

The pilot knew what was next. He nose-dived, scuttling away on his hands and knees, putting distance between himself and his former position. Several heartbeats later, a gaping hole exploded in the wall behind him, winging lethal stone fragments across the roof.

Ears ringing, Grimaldi armed the M-203 with another 40 mm shell. He came up, mentally gauging the distance, while braving the line of slugs that whined off stone. He pumped the 40 mm grenade, sent it flying straight and true toward the Lexus. The Stony Man pilot scored a direct hit as the vehicle turned into fiery scrap metal. At least two more gunmen checked out, all mangled arms and legs cartwheeling as they rode the blazing crest of the fireball.

Four down, two to go on the outside, but the survivors cut loose again with autofire, even as wreckage hammered the alley around them. They held their ground, determined to save the night.

As if to add insult and fury to that thought, the pilot found two more gunmen crouching on both sides of the warehouse door, joining their comrades in pinning Grimaldi as streams of autofire were hurled his way.

Staying low, Grimaldi raced for the far end of the factory roof, away from the storm of autofire. On the surface, the plan looked shot to hell, but he still had to try to take out the vehicles he knew would be racing out of the warehouse. No risk, no gain. No gain, no decisive victory.

Grimaldi only hoped Bolan was faring a little better. At this point, he could use a little help from his friend.

CHARGING IN BLIND while using the blasts to cover his entrance proved nearly fatal for Mack Bolan. It had been a gamble, no doubt, calling for lightning speed, brazenness and a steel will to drop the enemy before they knew what hit them.

Even though they were flinging it all back in his face with rapid response, Bolan had no choice but to run with the original play. To hesitate meant certain death.

The soldier never played it that way, and Bolan was well aware from the giving end that street fights were lost because an aggressor suddenly tucked his hands in his pockets when the going got tough, or generals rolled up the map and ordered a fighting withdrawal when one more forward thrust would have split the counterattack.

Not Bolan—not here, not now, not ever. One more thrust. It would be straight on, guns blazing, the meanest and quickest gun.

The soldier heard an explosion from beyond the warehouse and knew Grimaldi was going hard at it. It should shake the enemy up a little more at the least, get them scrambling to move out while Bolan drove them out into Grimaldi's gun sights.

Looking to take a live one for Q and A also became a long shot. Right then Bolan had his own survival problems.

He caught a break, though. He saw an opening between two rows of steel containers to his left flank. He ducked behind the steel barrier as the hardman ahead was hosing a long burst of autofire Bolan's way, bullets whining off steel beside the soldier. A glimpse to his side and he saw another gap between two more containers, dead ahead. He had a split second to act and was already holding back on the trigger of his M-16, firing as the bald giant popped into view ahead, anticipating the enemy's reemergence. Downrange the soldier's line of 5.56 mm slugs screeched off steel, driving Zharkov to cover.

Bolan plucked a frag grenade off his webbing, armed it and hurled it behind him as he slid into the cover between the two containers. They had met his surge with their own counterattack to outflank him. It had nearly succeeded, and still could. Bolan never went into an engagement underestimating the enemy. This time was no different. Only this time the enemy was proving a willingness to die to protect either their boss or whatever was in the warehouse.

Autofire again began rattling in the direction he had bolted from. Bolan thought he heard another blast shake the warehouse out front, but couldn't be sure because of the sound of weapons fire. The soldier was arming another frag grenade, crouching for deeper cover, when the first lethal egg blew. His effort was rewarded by a scream, followed by an abrupt end to weapons fire from that direction. Two heartbeats later, the soldier whirled low around the corner and gave the second frag grenade an underhand pitch, as the bald giant flung himself around the edge of the steel container, firing for all he was worth. Bolan glimpsed the assassin's eyes widen as the frag bomb bounced his way.

Riding out the second blast, as lethal steel fragments took to the air and screamed off steel, Bolan cracked a fresh 30-round magazine into his assault rifle. He broke cover, heading into the smoke of blast number two. If the giant popped into sight, he was dead. Bolan knew he was taking his chances, charging into the open, but he was adrenalized, sensing he had turned back the enemy's attack. Still, he kept alert and ready for any movement. Nothing appeared.

And Zharkov didn't show either, as Bolan, crouched low, wheeled around the corner of the container to the sounds of men yelling and engines racing dead ahead. Another explosion rocked the night as the flash of a fireball illuminated the darkness beyond the rolling door.

Bolan took in the chaos in an eye blink. The giant was up, slamming a new magazine into his AK-47, bellowing orders. Bolan glimpsed Gregor Drakovich already diving into the back seat of the lead luxury vehicle. As two gunmen fired upward with AKMs from the open doorway, the vehicle with Drakovich lurched ahead on a squeal of rubber, bulldozing through the fiery wreckage outside.

The rest of the enemy's escape was momentarily delayed by a vicious argument taking place near the remaining vehicle. It seemed three swarthy, bearded men were bickering with two soldiers. The hardmen dropped hands over the shoulders of two of the bickerers, tried to shove them into the car. One of them was holding the duffel bag Bolan had seen earlier, Smolenskov's bag, and the ex-KGB man was nowhere in sight. The dark trio had to be the atomic mules, the soldier figured. They wanted weapons, Bolan overheard. They wanted to fight.

"Get your asses in the car now or I'll shoot you where you stand!" Zharkov roared.

The giant then turned his grim attention Bolan's way, almost as if the soldier had been forgotten while he raged around the warehouse, kicking verbal ass.

Bolan seized advantage of the momentary lapse, already charging across a short stretch of no-man's-land, dropping behind to cover. With a better angle of fire now on his enemies, the Executioner came around the corner, finger curled around the M-203's trigger, and cut loose a 40 mm grenade on the vehicle where the bulk of the enemy had gathered.

The 40 mm grenade hammered into the side of the vehicle with maximum impact, producing a fireball and flying bodies that told Bolan his chances of taking a live one were next to zero.

Bolan caught momentary sight of a wounded figure. Zharkov had been knocked to the warehouse floor by the blast.

Bolan also saw the battle was far from over. The giant staggered to his feet, bloody and dazed, but bellowing Russian obscenities. Bolan held back on the M-16's trigger. Zharkov stood his ground, directing wild autofire Bolan's way even as a line of 5.56 mm slugs ripped up his chest. The giant held on, the AK-47 turned toward the ceiling, spitting out a final few rounds before Zharkov toppled on his back, twitched out in death throes, then lay utterly still.

From the open doorway leading to the alley, the two hardmen were now scrambling to their feet, having ducked the explosion. Their faces, streaked with blood from flying glass and metal, were outlined in firelight, making them clear targets. Grimaldi scored a head shot on one of the hardmen before Bolan expended what was left of his clip into the chest of the other goon.

With a fresh clip slapped into his M-16, Bolan fanned the warehouse in all directions. With the smell of blood and cordite in his nose, the crackle of fire in his ears, Bolan radioed Grimaldi.

"Wolf Runner, what's the situation?"

"You're clear out here. Watch your step over the bodies and wreckage on the way out. I'm scoping now. Nothing's moving. Definite clearance, Steel Talon, not even a twitch. Unfortunately, the bad guys held me down long enough to get one of the vehicles home free. Roadrunner one cleared."

Gregor Drakovich had made it. Worse, Bolan knew

the battle would bring the law running. It was time to clear out.

"Consolidate your gear in my vehicle. Then meet me out front on the double."

"Already moving. ETA two minutes. Wolf Runner, over and out."

One of the wounded men looked up at Bolan with pain and hate in his eyes. The blast had shredded the man's chest and face until he looked like nothing more than raw hamburger. Alert for any sounds of movement around him, Bolan loomed over the dying man.

"Why...who...who are you?"

Bolan stared down at the mutilated face. "Let's just say I'm not from the Red Cross." The soldier met those dying eyes with a cold and unforgiving stare. "Your Russian friends blew it, and you're not going to make it either. You want some payback, tell me what was happening here."

A bitter-sounding chuckle, then the wounded man sputtered, "Russians...betrayed us...Colonel...Tuhbat..."

Bolan filed away the name. "Were you moving uranium or plutonium waste from here?"

"We...go to Moscow...no...Russians...bastards didn't pay...no diamonds...exposed my men... radiation...liars..."

That was all Bolan got. Without even a glance over his shoulder, the Executioner moved out to meet Grimaldi.

ANOTHER BATTLE WON, but the war was only just beginning, the Executioner knew. With their enemies reeling, and grappling, no doubt, to make sense out of all the mayhem, it was no time to take things slowly.

There was one last stop to make before their business in Brighton Beach was wrapped up.

Grimaldi had the wheel of the Cadillac. From somewhere in the distance, Bolan caught the faint but growing wail of sirens. They were putting quick distance to the warehouse killzone but Bolan kept his eyes peeled, M-16 in his lap. He had given Grimaldi a quick update on what little he'd learned from the mule.

"So, we know at least one son is most likely hopping a flight for Moscow," Grimaldi said. "Minus three mules, minus the cash drop for services never to be rendered. And with the oldest Drakovich still out there, maybe circling the wagons right now with the old man. What's the plan, Sarge? Brighton Beach has gotten too hot."

Bolan knew Grimaldi was right. Their time was up in Brighton Beach. Sooner or later the FBI would be alerted to the war against the Russian Mafia. It wouldn't take the IQ of a genius for Winfrey or his superiors to figure out Special Agent Belasko was scything through the enemy ranks. When the FBI discovered they had been duped into letting Brighton Beach become a killing field, that window of time Bolan had been granted would slam shut.

"Now, we're going for the Don."

"DON'T GO TO the warehouse, do you hear me? Go directly to the airport and leave immediately with your brother."

Yuri Drakovich listened to his older son's protest. For a long moment, stunned by the report Vlad had given him—which he, in turn, had received from the Family's police captain—the banquet room seemed to

spin in the boss's eyes. Yuri Drakovich hit a heavy belt of vodka to make sure the room stayed still.

It was incredible, if what he had heard was true. Given all that had happened so far, though, he had no reason to doubt his son's report. Vlad was a proved and seasoned soldier, after all. He didn't panic. They were under siege. Apparently the mystery enemy wouldn't rest until the entire Drakovich Family was dead, and their operation nothing more than a shattered dream.

Yuri Drakovich had a strong suspicion the nameless enemy would come for him soon. In a way he was a sitting target in his restaurant, surrounded only by a small army of soldiers. Then again, a part of him hoped, silently dared his nameless enemy to come to him, face-to-face, to finish it.

Perhaps it was seeing, dealing so much death and destruction in his lifetime that gave him some uncanny sixth sense that the end was near. Whatever, he wanted nothing more right then than to make sure his sons were safe, homeward bound to Russia. The success of the operation was far more important than even his own life, he decided. If he died that night, then he at least had two heirs to carry on.

"Be quiet!" Drakovich barked into the phone. "Do what I tell you! Go to the airport. Our private jet is fueled and ready to go. We have an ongoing operation that must prevail at all costs. Too much is at stake. Listen to me! The information you will need to carry on the operation is in my floor safe at the dacha." He gave his son the combination. "No matter what happens you are to see the operation through to its conclusion. Am I clear?"

The father listened to the heavy pause on the other

end. He felt sick to his stomach, as if he sensed his son also knew the end was in sight. Then Vlad, in a strange, distant voice, said, "Father, I don't like what I'm hearing. You sound as if you think whoever is attacking us is coming there and will kill you. You make it sound as if you don't plan on—"

"What I plan to do or not is of no consequence to you or your brother. Shut up and listen! If something should happen to me, you are to take over the Family."

"Father, I don't like this, I'm coming there right away—"

"No! If you disobey me on this, I'll never forgive you. Do you understand me, Vlad?" A hard silence. "Vlad?"

"Very well."

"That's all. Contact me when you arrive in Moscow," he said, and heard the note of fear in his voice.

He hung up, hating the hollow sound of uncertainty of his last words. He looked at Sergei Vuraylev, asked, "How many men are on the premises?"

The soldier said, "Thirteen."

Drakovich grunted. "I'm glad I'm not given to American superstition," he said with a chuckle.

Just then the door opened, and Drakovich read the look of fear and confusion on the face of the soldier, an ex-Spetsnaz commando he knew as Constantin Yurabov.

Drakovich fired up a cigarette, waiting. "What is it? Speak!"

The Mob boss listened as the soldier informed him someone, a man, had just telephoned. The stranger said to relay a message to the boss.

He grew more angry as the soldier hesitated. "And? Goddamm it, what?"

"He said to tell you that you're closed for business

for the night. That you are to clear the restaurant of all noncombatants. If he walks in and sees even a busboy you will, uh...you will be made to feel..."

He heard the rest. This bastard, he thought to himself. Oh, he had balls, all right, this American shooter. And just who was he?

Rage burned hot through his blood. This was unbelievable. This didn't happen to the man who had come to America in search of the good life, and for his sons no less. He owned the American police, judges and lawyers. He owned Brighton Beach. People looked at him with respect. Now he was being hunted like an animal, and on his own turf, right before his own people, kicked around as if he was nothing more than dog shit. It was beyond outrage and disrespect. It was sacrilege. He would avenge the blood of the men he had lost, save face and watch this American die slowly and in great pain.

"This bastard," Drakovich suddenly roared, striding for the weapons hanging on a rack in the wall compartment. "Let him come then! Let this American dog walk right in here! Clear the place, run everyone who isn't one of us the hell out of here! Let's see just how big his balls really are!" Drakovich screamed, hurling a stream of profanity in all directions, cursing every man and his mother and God under the sun.

Drakovich didn't just take any weapon. Rather, he grabbed an HK-11 light machine gun, chambered for 7.62 mm bullets. He took an 80-round drum and attached it to the lmg. "Let this pig bastard walk right in here, do you understand! I want to look him right in the eye before I kill him!"

It was all Drakovich could do to keep from unleashing the machine gun. But he would wait. If nothing else, if he was going to die, he would die on his feet.

7

They were waiting, but Bolan had expected as much. Bad news certainly traveled fast, and he strongly suspected his phone call to the restaurant had further shaken up the ranks.

Crouched low in the corner of an alley that ran behind the restaurant, Uzi submachine gun poised to fire, the Executioner watched the lone sentry with an AKM assault rifle slung around his shoulder. The hardman was pacing, all nerves and tension. The gunner was looking all around, and Bolan ducked back out of sight before roving eyes searched his way.

With the attack plan on the table, Bolan and Grimaldi had already done a drive-by of Brighton Beach Avenue, two of the surrounding blocks, reconning at the Bear's Head. The Drakovich restaurant appeared deserted, a faint glow of light beaconing from inside the plate-glass window, but Bolan knew better, could damn near smell the fear and desperation of men waiting like cornered animals inside the place. He couldn't be sure how many enemies they would face, but both warriors were prepared to tackle a small army with overwhelming and massive firepower. Strike first, and hit harder than the enemy.

It was well after midnight, and under normal circumstances Brighton Beach Avenue would have been jumping with drinkers and dancers despite the chill in the air. The streets were now nearly empty of late-night revelers.

Peeking around the corner, the soldier assessed the situation as the sentry turned his focus on the mouth of the alley, unaware he was marked for doom. The back service door to the restaurant was wide open. Bolan suspected he was being invited in to face the music. Fair enough. Most likely the boss was tired of riding it out, nerves frayed while his troops were out there dying, his business deal shot to hell, warehouse demolished, police right then picking through the wreckage, maybe en route to question Drakovich. Bolan believed the Don wanted it finished, one way or another.

It was dicey, Bolan knew, going in for a full frontal assault but the Stony Man soldiers played the game hard. The original shopping list pretty much went out the window during Bolan's encounter with Smolenskov anyway. If the Russians were stepping up the timetable for their own agenda then the Executioner had no choice but to do likewise. Either way, Brighton Beach had become way too hot. It was time to move out.

First the Boss.

Slinging the Uzi around his shoulder, Bolan drew the Beretta 93-R, and attached the sound-suppressor. He checked his chronometer. Grimaldi would be making his way on foot to the front door, M-16 in hand.

Bolan steadied his aim in a two-handed grip, drawing a bead on the sentry's head with the weapon before slipping his finger around the trigger. The range was a little more than thirty feet.

The sentry was turning Bolan's way when the Beretta chugged out a 9 mm Parabellum round. The Executioner scored a head shot. With the sentry falling,

Bolan moved out, stepping past the body, his gun poised in the direction of the service door. If the crunch of deadweight alarmed anyone inside and sent them running Bolan was ready to cut loose.

Low beside the door Bolan looked inside. Gloomy light shone from around the corner at the end of the hallway. The way in looked clear. The soldier didn't trust the silence.

He leathered the Beretta, unslung the SMG, then forged into the hall, adrenalized, ready to cut down anything that made a move his way. He checked the ceiling for minicams but if they were there he couldn't see them. Reaching the end of the hall, he crouched.

He had come to another hallway. Off to one side he saw that the hall led to the swinging double doors of the kitchen. In the other direction it led into the main dining room.

And there he spotted two shadows with assault rifles, hunched behind tables, looking toward the front door.

Another quick glance at his chronometer and Bolan knew Grimaldi was seconds away from hitting the main entrance.

Bolan took and armed a frag grenade. He pitched it out into the dining room. When the steel egg hit the floor and rolled on, the sound made a racket in the utter silence and alerted the troops.

The soldier was up and moving as voices shouted in alarm. He was about to spray the main dining room with his Uzi when a voice shouted from behind a door in the hallway. A second later all hell broke loose as an unseen enemy began screaming from behind the door, "Come on, you bastard! Show yourself!"

The grenade blew in the main dining room but Bolan was forced to duck when sudden autofire lashed the air and gaping holes were punched through the door by his side.

GRIMALDI WAS DROPPING to the pavement, scuttling forward in a belly-crawl for the front door when he heard the shouting beyond the plate glass. Then the night rocked on with a sudden blast. Bolan was inside and making his move.

Time to get busy.

As if the enemy was daring him to come in, Grimaldi saw the front door was slightly ajar. With his M-16 set on full-auto, the Stony Man pilot decided to oblige his enemies.

He was up and running, bursting through the front door, intent on taking any and all comers. On the way in, he was greeted by the smells of blood and cordite, and glimpsed two mangled bodies strewed on the main dining room floor around a pair of tables that had been reduced to matchsticks by the frag bomb.

In the soft sheen of light coming from several table lamps Grimaldi sought out targets, picked out two shadows directing weapons fire toward a hallway in the opposite direction. On the fly, the pilot sprayed the room, his long burst of 5.56 mm lead stitching up the sides of his first two targets.

He saw two goons by the bar, cursing and shouting, not sure which way to turn. Grimaldi answered their uncertainty, pumping out a 40 mm grenade from his M-203. He ducked as the explosion, deafening in the tight confines of the dining room, took out the bar and the two hardmen in flash of fire. Screams of pain knifed the air as flying glass shrapnel found flesh.

Grimaldi saw Bolan pouring it on with his Uzi, sweeping the dining room where several shadows were popping over tables and directing return autofire the Executioner's way. The enemy was spinning all around, caught now in a pincer squeeze of flying lead.

Grimaldi cracked home a fresh clip into his M-16, then dropped behind a glass-mirrored pillar. Several rounds shattered the glass. He gritted his teeth as fragments slapped his face, then he burned the entire clip into the backsides of the two gunmen downrange. They yelled in pain and surprise. The enemy spun again, only this time in death.

Grimaldi heard another furious barrage of automatic fire, but couldn't pinpoint right away from where it was unleashed. Then he saw a door flung open, dead ahead. A tall figure with an AK-47 appeared in the doorway and began firing, rattling off a long burst around the room.

The lone shooter almost got lucky, driving Grimaldi for cover behind the pillar again while slugs blasted off hunks of glass over the pilot's head. Grimaldi slapped another fresh magazine into his assault rifle. A glimpse around the opposite corner of the pillar, and he knew he had to act. He realized he was pinned down by the relentless barrage of autofire until he spotted Bolan going to work with a frag grenade.

"COME ON, AMERICAN, show yourself! It's just you and me!"

Bolan heard the cursing and the ravings between the long bursts of gunfire slicing up the doorway directly behind him. The soldier had never spoken to the Boss of Brighton Beach, couldn't possibly recognize the voice, but instinct warned him Yuri Drakovich was in the room, hell-bent on making his last stand.

Moments ago, Bolan saw he needed to help pave the

way for Grimaldi. Now that they were both in, scything down the enemy, it was time for the mop-up.

The Executioner heard the roar of autofire from around the corner. The shooter had Grimaldi pinned at the far end of the dining room. Bolan grabbed his second-to-last frag grenade, armed it, wheeled low around the corner and gave it an underhand lob. No sooner was the steel egg bouncing away than the soldier took his last frag grenade, pulled the pin and dropped the spoon. He pulled back to cover, caught a glimpse through the shattered ruins of the side door of a face of pure rage. And he recognized Yuri Drakovich from his intel pack.

The Boss was twenty feet or so inside the room, holding back the trigger of a light machine gun with a drum barrel, sweeping the door, the wall, going for broke in a blind fury.

Bolan tossed the frag bomb through the gaping hole as the thunder of an explosion shook the air ahead. A brief scream of agony, and he didn't have to look to know Grimaldi's shooter had just been blown out of the picture.

When his last grenade detonated Bolan paused for several heartbeats while countless steel bits razored around the room beyond, clearing the way for him. Then he barreled through the jagged teeth of the doorway. He hit the floor, rolled, came up, Uzi in hand.

Cordite choking his senses, Bolan caught the sounds of gagging from beyond the cloud. Off to his side, he saw Grimaldi hit a crouch beside the red ruins of the corpse in the smoking maw of the doorway. Two figures staggered to their feet in Bolan's sights. They had spotted the grenade, made a run for it. They were dazed and bloodied but the fight was hardly kicked out of them.

At the same time, Bolan and Grimaldi cut loose with new rounds.

The first gunner toppled into a Jacuzzi under the combined burst from the Stony Man team, flailing limbs throwing up a splash that was part water, part crimson. Bolan tracked on, glimpsing the snarling face of Yuri Drakovich in a far corner. The big table in the middle of the room had taken the brunt of the grenade blast, shielding the Boss from certain death. Even so, Drakovich was a bloody mess from flying shrapnel.

And the Don was going out like a lion. The light machine gun turned Bolan's way, Drakovich roaring out a stream of profanity, rattling out a short burst before twin streams of autofire marched across the Boss's chest. The light machine gun went silent and Drakovich dropped from sight.

A quick scan of the room, and Bolan found no one left to fight. He gave Grimaldi the nod and they backed out the door.

For a long moment, cautious, poised to fire, both men gave the carnage in the dining room a hard search. Nothing moved. Not even a groan or a twitch of bloody limbs.

"Back door," Bolan told Grimaldi. "Time to fly."

THEY WERE ROLLING down Brighton Beach Avenue with Grimaldi at the wheel of the Cadillac. As they passed the abattoir that was the Bear's Head, Bolan gave their surroundings a long scan. The racket had brought a few of the curious out in the dark, but no one seemed nosy enough to check the killzone. He didn't even catch the sound of a distant siren.

Ahead, Bolan saw the island block where the Russian Mafia had erected their business fronts at the expense of former owners. Grimaldi drove on slowly, one eye on the rearview mirror.

"Where to, Sarge?"

"The jet."

"I'll touch base with the Farm," Grimaldi said. "Make sure the way is smoothed out. I assume we're flying to Moscow?"

"Yeah."

Bolan found the sidewalk along the short stretch of Mafia buildings clear of late-night stragglers. No better time than the present, as they were riding out, to put the big bang to the night. As Grimaldi drove past the lonely buildings, he took the remote control, offered it to Bolan.

"You want the honors?"

"You did the dirty work."

A thin smile formed as Grimaldi settled his thumb over the button.

SOMEHOW YURI DRAKOVICH found the resolve to stand. He was beyond anger and shock, pain or outrage. He was dying hard and fast and there wasn't a damn thing he could do about it. He gritted his teeth, shuffling ahead, kicking through a carpet of glass and wood shards. He burned from head to foot, wasn't even sure how many bullets had torn through him, but the fire in his body told him he was still alive. He had been shot before. Pain was good, but he knew within minutes he would bleed out, shock setting in, warm, then cold...

He staggered from the ruins of the banquet room. He choked on his own blood and heard the awful wheezing in his ears as he fought to breathe. A hole in his lung would soon be the least and last of his worries.

He stood in the eerie and all-powerful silence. It was a mind-boggling sight, the ruins of his restaurant, the dead sprawled before him.

Drakovich cursed. The two Americans had prevailed, at least for the moment. He had failed, but he knew he wasn't defeated.

His sons were still out there, and they would avenge this horror.

He was stumbling forward, not sure what to do, or where he could find a suitable place among the smoking ruins to die.

Drakovich kicked something. Looking down, he choked on bitter laughter at the sight of the full and unbroken bottle of vodka.

He bent, groaning, and picked up the bottle. He looked through the plate-glass window. It was dark and very still beyond the restaurant. No one was coming, no one ventured to look inside. He was alone.

Earlier he had spread the word out on the streets. Everyone was to go home, stay inside, all restaurants in the area closed for business. And he had informed his paid police captain to not come running if someone phoned in a report of gunfire in the area. Of course, the police would arrive in short order. But they would be left with only questions, standing there in the ruins and gaping around in shock and disbelief.

It was over.

Drakovich found an undamaged chair facing the window. He could at least greet whoever came through the door first. A vision of death, sitting upright, bottle in hand. It was an odd picture to form in his mind but it hung there just the same.

The Don sat, waiting. The American bastards were good, he thought. Wild men who could shoot and kill, blow up the opposition, then move on. If only he had a half dozen like them....

Yuri Drakovich felt the warmth creeping over him, the pain fading. He uncapped the bottle, raised it toward the dark street.

"To my enemies," he growled, and took a deep swallow that washed the blood, burning down his chest. "You will soon join me in hell."

8

Igor Pavlovka had always hated the heat, stink and noise of Aden. A perpetual assault on his senses, it never failed to stoke a fire in his belly, a fire that could only be doused, he knew, with the smell of enemy blood in his nose and on his hands from torture and killing.

The former KGB assassin had spent a large part of the past quarter-century in what used to be the PDRY—the People's Democratic Republic of Yemen—and he always wanted to believe he could adjust to the hellish inferno of heat and noise of the port city. He never had, and he figured he never would. Perhaps it was best that way, all the discomfort and agitation keeping him mean, sharp and ready for action.

When the Marxist Arab state shed the armor of its fanatical Communist stance and joined hands—at least on paper—with North Yemen to become the Republic of Yemen, Pavlovka had been forced, along with small armies of Russian military advisers and other KGB officers and assassins, to pull up stakes, flee the country until the dust settled.

Quickly it all went back to business as usual. Which meant the military advisers, operatives and assassins returned, even with the fall of communism and the new dawn rising over democratic Russia. Of course, by then they were all former KGB or ex-Spetsnaz but they were hardly out of work. The burgeoning, all-pervasive Russian Mafia had seen their talents were well used, for which they gained rewards far richer than the state's meager handouts during the Communist days.

Indeed, they had set something in motion, a little more than two decades ago, that could not be reversed. And Pavlovka and his new business associates in Moscow and the United States were the architects of something that would put Yemen on the map. If he and his associates proved the catalysts for a major war in the Middle East, he didn't care. By then, he and his partners would be long gone, rich men, safely entrenched somewhere far away, spending their millions, laughing while these countries hurled missiles back and forth, turning their nations into glowing rubble.

Pavlovka lifted the bottle of vodka off the nightstand and took a deep pull. He ran a casual eye over the AK-47s slung from the shoulders of the lean, dark-skinned Yemenis, noted the *jambiyas,* the universal Arab curved daggers sheathed inside black sashes. It was believed there were sixty million firearms in the country. He had done more than his fair share of bringing everything from AKs and hand grenades to Stingers into Yemen. It was definitely a plus, he thought, that any man could go anywhere in Yemen, armed to the teeth, and not get stopped or questioned by the authorities. Of course a foreigner would have to grease the right palms if he was to roam about, armed to kill.

Either way, it made doing business in Yemen that much easier. Pavlovka's own AKM was resting on a small round table, within easy reach. He also felt reassured by the weight of the 9 mm Makarov pistol in shoulder holster, and on his hip was a sheathed commando dagger. It wasn't nearly as big or as fearsome as the Arab *jambiya,* but Pavlovka had proved himself more than capable of using the blade.

The scar-faced terrorist Pavlovka knew as Sharif fidgeted in the lingering silence. Finally he said, "Perhaps, Comrade Pavlovka, you should persuade your boy to switch from heroin to qat or even share some of your vodka that you have smuggled into Yemen. His problem is disgusting, to say the least. And my employer is experiencing much discomfort, not to mention a whole lot of unnecessary paranoia because of your boy's addiction. As you know, alcohol alone is illegal for Muslims to consume in Yemen. What do you think would happen to the man we work for if the authorities discover he's a major distributor of narcotics?"

Pavlovka grunted as he sipped some illegal vodka. He unfolded his muscular bulk, pleased to see he dwarfed the Yemenis by nearly a foot as he rose to his full six-and-a-half feet. With the back of a meaty hand, he wiped sweat off his heavily bristled square jaw, then sent beads of moisture flying from his long black hair when he shook his head.

"Correct me if I'm wrong, but I believe," Pavlovka said, "that chewing qat is considered a social event. It's done in dens, at parties, in the *mafraj* of Yemeni houses. You people take the Spanish version of a siesta in the middle of the afternoon, desert the streets in hordes to go chew together. I don't believe my boy is a social creature. I also believe he is far beyond the mild narcotic effects of mere qat chewing. Now, if that is all..."

"Don't patronize us," Sharif growled. "I'm here to warn you in no uncertain terms. Rabiya is very angry.

He's in danger of being exposed because of your boy. Your Saudi prince has become an embarrassment, sending out his cronies, banging on doors in the middle of the night, disturbing Rabiya at his various business functions, these Saudis looking and acting all desperate and crazed. His increasing risk involves increasing the payments."

"How much?"

"It's something he wishes to discuss personally with you."

Pavlovka couldn't keep the wry smile off his face. "And if I tell him I don't care if they march him right out to the nearest square and lop off his head?"

"That would be most unwise. Rabiya has many eyes and ears in Aden and beyond. He suspects what you and your minions of Muscovite comrades, your *Mafiya* comrades I might add, are doing here in Yemen. All he has to do is put out the word to the American embassy, which, as you know, is merely a CIA way station. I'm sure you wouldn't want the CIA shadowing your every move in Yemen."

They already were, but Pavlovka wasn't about to tell him that.

"I further suggest you tell your Saudi prince he no longer seek out Rabiya by himself or through his Hezbollah cronies. Rabiya will give him what he needs through me. That is, if you agree to the new price. And it won't be in your worthless rubles."

Pavlovka laid a mean grin on the Yemeni. "My worthless rubles, eh? Okay, how about I pay him then in your even more worthless dinars or riyals?"

"Cash, American dollars!" Sharif roared. "Don't play with us on this!"

Pavlovka showed them a strange smile, then quietly

said, "Never. I'm not a man to play games." He looked at his watch. "Very well. Two hours exactly. There's a qat den off King Solomon Street."

"I know the place."

"Is that good enough for your man?"

"Yes. Two hours. Don't be late."

"I regret that this has all become so unpleasant."

The Yemenis spun on their heels and strode for the door. Sharif grabbed the knob, then added, "See that it doesn't become even more unpleasant. A gift of much American dollars would go a long way in making it all better."

When he was alone, Pavlovka said to himself, "I assure you, it will be pleasant."

Pavlovka hit the bottle one more time. Then he went to the window, pulled back the drape, feeling some of that paranoia the Yemeni had mentioned. Below the market stalls were a cluster of brightly garbed Yemenis hawking their wares, the streets cluttered with camels and dogs, taxis and old model cars alike. It was dusty, dirty and overcrowded down there, with man, animal and machine baking under a raging sun. In that crowd, he couldn't pick out a CIA agent with a long search from his fourth-floor window, but if he was on the street he could, simply because his life would depend on it.

Now this petty drug business was adding to the tension. Well, he would deal with it, and in the only logical way he knew how. When a thorn was stuck in the side, the only thing to do was to remove it.

Pavlovka moved from the window to the dresser. There, he pulled a laptop computer from a drawer. It displayed a small radio console that provided a secure and direct line to a number in Moscow. He checked his watch. The call was hours late. Something was wrong. His instinct for trouble had never failed him. And his survival always depended on accurate information, concrete details about how to proceed with an operation, to ensure it was foolproof.

He wanted to believe that no news from Moscow was good news. But Igor Pavlovka had a sick feeling in his gut. He sweated, drank some more vodka and heard a voice in his head that warned him this was going to be a long day.

IF PATIENCE was a virtue Pavlovka thought someday they would canonize him Saint Igor, patron saint of patience. He almost smiled at the image of popes and bishops and whoever else crowning him, his name spoken in reverence, his memory nothing but an honor no mere mortal could ever live up to. The fantasy kept him going for the moment, and dreams were good in a way. A man who didn't dream had nothing to live for because he had no ambition to become something better, something more. But to see dreams come true required action.

And all he wanted right then was quick and decisive action. He had a dream, all right, but he had troubles, too. All the problems and worries dumped in his lap, all the bartering and money deliveries to shore up, all the egos of key bidders to massage, and he was now forced to waste the better part of the day on some very unpleasant business.

With his AKM slung from his shoulder, he walked out of his room, leaving it guarded by one of his men. Two more ex-Spetsnaz commandos with AK-47s marched in step with Pavlovka to the room at the end of the hall. He came to the door but didn't knock. He just turned the knob and rolled in.

The two Hezbollah terrorists leaped to their feet, all snarls and curses. The one he knew as Mohammed said, "Don't you know how to knock!"

"Shut up and leave the room. Both of you! Now!"

He read the defiance and hesitation in their dark eyes. Pavlovka pulled the rifle off his shoulder, held it low by his side, ready to go if they even twitched too much.

"If I have to repeat myself it won't be good," Pavlovka said. "And whatever it is you're thinking, I'd urge you to reconsider. Your prince wouldn't be happy if you piss on his deal in a stupid moment."

After fidgeting and scowling, they left, escorted out of the room by Pavlovka's men. When the door banged shut it took a long moment for the Russian to adjust his eyes to the gloomy light.

In the far dark corner of the room Pavlovka saw him. He looked at the emaciated figure stretched out on the white mattress. The Russian snorted, disgusted at the sight of a man who had had it all not long ago before he threw it away. The scarecrow lying there in soiled underpants, ribs jutting against white skin, drool trickling out of its mouth, certainly didn't strike Pavlovka as any prince worth fifty million dollars.

Shouldering his weapon, Pavlovka grabbed a wooden chair. He took his bottle from his pants pocket and settled the chair by the bed, then sat. He saw the hypodermic needle, tourniquet, spoon and the Ziploc bag bulging with white powder on the nightstand. From the candlelight flickering over Prince Ali al-Aziz Kalbah's pale, gaunt face, Pavlovka saw the Saudi pry

open his eyes, a weird smile on his lips. The prince
was floating in smack heaven.

"You...my Russian protector and comrade...
where...my suitcase from Allah...my dream...
the deliverer of my vengeance..."

The prince nodded off.

This was weakness, self-pity beyond redemption to
the former KGB assassin. Pavlovka took a drink of
vodka, squished it around in his mouth, then spat it all
over Kalbah's face. "Wake up!"

The prince muttered a curse, stirred, then slapped at
his face. Anger flared in his eyes.

"Where's our money?"

Kalbah shivered. His beard and shoulder-length
black hair were matted with sweat. He stank like a pig,
and Pavlovka noted the Saudi's room was twice the
inferno he had just left. This new assault of stink and
heat was making Pavlovka very angry.

"The money!"

"I told you. I had it sent for. Swiss...land." Kalbah
struggled up on an elbow. "You know what has happened to me. I'm an outcast, a prince who could have
been king. I'd have been the leader of the Arab world!
I can still be that king of kings!" he roared, then cursed
like a demon in Arabic.

"Oh, yes. You stood to inherit the Khawahr oil
fields. Big shot. Spare me your pathetic history."

"Over eighty billion barrels. Eighty billion barrels!
They were mine. All mine!"

"And you pissed your future away for some dope."

"What do you know?" Kalbah snarled. "Do you
know who you are talking to, Russian?"

"A drug addict, a parasite."

"I am Prince Ali al-Aziz Kalbah! I am a direct descendant of the house of Saud! You are nothing more than a Russian killer!''

"Right now I'm all that stands between you and death, and you'll bow and scrape to me as if I was the fucking Prophet himself! Shut up and listen to me! You have been jerking me around for two months and I am a eye blink away from killing you and all your Hezbollah flunkies! I don't care how you feel cheated and how you want so desperately what we have so you can destroy those oil fields you will now never inherit! I don't give a shit that you lie and jerk off your Hezbollah cronies about how you'll be the one to vaporize your holy shrines of Mecca and Medina! I have real and serious problems, you sniveling, jet-setting, drug-addicted maggot puke. The least of which is that the man I work for wants to know whether you are in or out. Well?''

The Saudi paused. He seemed to shrivel before Pavlovka's sudden outburst. "It takes time to come up with twenty million dollars. My father froze three of my accounts. The one in Switzerland was all that I had left!''

"You had better hope he didn't also freeze that one.''

"My associates will be flying in...what is today?''

Pavlovka told him what day it was. "My Saudi friend, I hope you understand that twenty million may not be enough.''

"Yes,'' he rasped. "Your bidding war. I'm sure you do not threaten your Somali warlord or the Pakistanis like this.''

Pavlovka picked up the bag of dope and saw panic flash in the Saudi's eyes as he held it up. "I don't treat them like this because they aren't junkies. And because they have already shown me a possible down payment."

The prince tried brazen, which he didn't wear well. "You sought me out, I didn't come to you."

That was true, Pavlovka thought. When the project was in full swing and it looked as if completion would become reality the Boss had made a list of potential buyers who would have the money, the means and the determination to use what they were selling. They knew there would always be plenty of terrorists, cartels and dictators around who would froth at the mouth at the chance to buy what they had created. Of course, over several years, the list was narrowed down to those men who were serious enough and capable of coming up with the necessary money. A bidding war now existed. Indeed, the final and deadly serious hour was upon them all. It was time for the prince to shit or get off the pot.

Pavlovka opened the Ziploc bag, brutally delved out a small handful of powder, dumped it on the nightstand, then wiped off his hand on the mattress. "Listen to me. Wake up!" The prince nodded, eyelids fluttering shut until Pavlovka slapped him in the face. "You're to dry out as best you can until I see the money. If your cronies run with your money—"

"I trust them completely! They want what I want."

"What they want as opposed to what you want is debatable. That said, your life is your own, and I personally don't care if you live or die because of this garbage. I'll hold this," he said, pocketing the Ziploc bag and standing, "until I see your offer. If you squawk now, if you give me any crap at all, I'll flush this down the toilet. There is more, Prince, more problems you created for me. What you don't know or maybe don't care is that I have to go now and clean up a mess you created.''

"Radiya?"

"Yes. Radiya. Your prophet. Time is running out. While you get high and think how unkind and unfair life has been to you, the last of our bidders will be arriving within two days. If you don't have our money...."

Pavlovka let it hang, wheeled and walked away.

He heard panic hit the air as the prince cried out, "I'll have your money! But I can't fall ill! What am I to do if I need more?"

Pavlovka showed a cruel smile. "You Arabs are good at bowing, I understand. You know where my room is. I expect much bowing and scraping in the days to come."

He heard the prince's vicious curses lash his back as he left the room. Tough. Pavlovka was in control. The deal was about to go down, and he would soon be rich.

All that in mind, he decided maybe it wouldn't be such a bad day after all.

THE SECOND ORDER of business would be more pleasure than business, or so Pavlovka envisioned.

He was prepared to take care of the drug dealer and whoever else stood in his way. With Alexi and Sergei on his heels, he walked through the back door and handed the proprietor of the qat den a fat wad of American money. Pavlovka was late, but he had to make the necessary phone calls to smooth the way. First to the owner of the den, secondly to the authorities in Aden he had bought and paid for. It turned out no one gave a damn if Rabiya lived or died.

Beneath his light windbreaker, drenched in sweat,

Pavlovka carried a 9 mm Makarov pistol with attached sound-suppressor. His two ex-Spetsnaz hitters had likewise shed the heavier firepower. With a little bit of luck and a whole lot of balls, Pavlovka should be in and out in less than thirty seconds.

The proprietor handed the duffel bag and burlap sack to Sergei. "Private room in the back, left at the end of the hall. Rabiya and two others," Pavlovka heard the proprietor tell him, then he walked down the short and gloomy hallway.

Beyond the beaded curtain he heard laughter and loud talk, smelled cigarette and cigar smoke. This particular den, he knew, sold illegal alcohol and played American rock and roll. Aden was a city where almost every manner of foreigner could be found. And Pavlovka caught a glimpse of the whole spectrum of the human rainbow as he swept through the beaded curtains. He didn't make eye contact with any of the patrons.

Dead ahead, Pavlovka saw Sharif standing guard by the private room. Sharif looked at his watch, scowled and told Pavlovka, "You're late."

"I had to stop to acquire a gift for your boss. You do remember the gift you mentioned?"

Sharif didn't know how to take that, frowning as he looked past Pavlovka at the two Russians, then wheeled through the beaded curtain.

In a heartbeat, Pavlovka took in the small room, as he followed the Yemeni into the private den. Sharif, the other Yemeni he knew as Mohammed and a small figure with a goatee and long black hair were sitting at a round table. Rabiya had his back to the wall, sipping from a glass filled with a dark liquid. He was all scowls and indignant looks until he realized what was happening. And too late.

The two ex-Spetsnaz hitters had their Makarovs out and chugging as soon they swept through the beaded curtain.

Pavlovka heard the muffled retorts of the sound-suppressed pistols. Out of the corner of his eye he glimpsed Sharif taking two rounds to the back of the head. Sharif was flung into the wall facefirst, a crimson smear rolling down the white stone wall. The other Yemeni nearly had the AK-47 off his shoulder but he never fired a shot as two more rounds punched through his forehead.

Pavlovka grabbed the edge of the table with one hand. He thrust it forward, ramming the edge deep into Rabiya's stomach. The air belched from the heroin dealer's gaping mouth as he was pinned to the wall. Pavlovka jammed the nose of the Makarov under Rabiya's chin. Beside Pavlovka the large burlap sack was dumped on the table.

Without hesitation, without a word, Pavlovka squeezed the trigger twice. Blood sprayed the wall behind Rabiya as his shattered skull hammered stone. Even before Pavlovka backed away from the table, Sergei had grabbed one of the *jambiyas*, moved and bent over Rabiya. He lifted the blade.

DUFFEL BAG IN HAND, Pavlovka burst into the room. The prince's cronies were leaping to their feet but Sergei and Alexi aimed their assault rifles at them, freezing them in midjump.

Pavlovka strode toward the prince, who was in the same outstretched position. But Kalbah sat up suddenly, coming alive with anger in his eyes. Pavlovka dumped the duffel bag in the Saudi's lap. Outrage was flung all around, as the cronies demanded to know what was going on, their weapons seized by Pavlovka's hitters.

"Open it," Pavlovka ordered.

"What is this?"

The Russian repeated his command. Slowly the prince zipped open the duffel bag. He stared inside the bag, then removed the burlap sack, his eyes widening with horror as blood dripped onto his legs.

"Two days, prince. Have our money or be gone."

Pavlovka turned as the Saudi looked into the sack. As he headed for the door he heard the cry of anguish, then the flood of curses lashing his back. He had no time, no patience for the Saudi's weakness. His point was made.

As Pavlovka entered his room, he found Alexander Maryov at the laptop.

"A moment, he just arrived."

It was the call Pavlovka had been waiting for. He took the headset from Maryov and slipped it on. He took the mike and said, "Yes."

The familiar voice of his longtime comrade and business associate came on, speaking in Russian. He listened as Vasily Smolenskov said, "Comrade, I'm afraid we may have a problem. The Boss is dead."

9

"It feels wrong, Sarge. I've got this itch between my shoulder blades I can't scratch. That usually means I'm lined up in someone's cross hairs. I mean, I didn't expect us to be greeted with open arms by the joint CIA-FSK contacts as soon as we disembarked from the jet. But I think I could have done without Captain Mikhail Pushkin of the Foreign Counterintelligence Service. Hell, we could have gotten more on the Drakovich operations here in Moscow from the ghost of Stalin. They didn't give us a damn thing other than a few addresses, which we could have gotten from the Farm. You read this the way I do, Sarge? The Drakovich Family is protected."

Bolan was watching the black ZIL limousine three blocks ahead. Inside the limo were three hardmen and one of their main targets. Grimaldi was at the wheel of their sedan rental, also monitoring their surroundings, while maintaining cautious distance from their quarry.

At the moment Bolan silently admitted he was feeling the effects of the transatlantic flight, the tension, agitation and prebattle nerves, just like his friend. But it was gut check time. Both of them knew they would have to dig deep, stay razor-sharp and grimly prepare to meet the unknown with all the martial skills and raw determination they could muster to take down the enemy.

Too many critical hours had passed since Bolan and Grimaldi had touched down at a remote airfield, just north of Sheremetyevo International Airport. International protocol and intel gathering on the part of the Stony Man warriors had slowed their pace, while Bolan knew their enemies were out there regrouping, laying out their next move. According to Brognola, the clandestine airstrip where their customized Grumman Gulfstream Lear Jet was now grounded was jointly owned by the CIA and the FSK. More of the new and improved East-West relations in bloom, Bolan thought. Since shortly after the end of the Cold War Bolan knew the CIA and the newer and kinder version of the KGB supposedly worked together on internal problems, such as domestic terrorism and other various conspiracies by rebel factions to overthrow the democratic government in Russia. But after the hostility and stonewalling Grimaldi referred to the soldier wasn't sure who was who and what was what.

Not that it mattered. They were on Russian soil to bring the war to the enemy's home turf. Even still, for "special agents" of the Justice Department to get clearance to operate in Russia, heavily armed no less, Bolan knew Brognola would have them touch base with the Foreign Counterintelligence Service, along with a CIA rep from the U.S. embassy.

"The good Captain of the FSK acted—and the operative word is acted—as if he didn't know or didn't give a damn about the atomic mules the Russian Mafia is flying all over the world. He pretty much hinted the Drakovich Family is untouchable, like they're some kind of royalty, modern czars."

Bolan let Grimaldi talk, figuring his friend was bone-tired from jetting them from New York to Moscow. Not to mention the frayed nerves and flowing adrenaline, as they marched into the uncertainty of the new battlefront, with no support and the possibility of being shadowed by the FSK or CIA, who could throw down a stumbling block at any moment.

What Grimaldi said was true, and Bolan gave it a moment's thought as he watched the limo roll on through the night, southbound, following the curve of the Moscow River along Lenin Prospekt. Then he checked his side-view mirror again. No vehicle appeared to be tailing them, but Bolan wasn't taking anything for granted.

For starters, the FSK most likely knew about the Drakovich operations, perhaps even knew the location of the nuclear power plants from which uranium, plutonium and possibly other component parts for a nuclear reactor were being smuggled out of the country. From past experience working with Russian counter-intelligence he knew the FSK were embarrassed that their nuclear reactors, even nuclear missile stockpiles, were being raided.

But the bottom line was Bolan and Grimaldi were on their own, as had been pointed out earlier by the FSK captain. Further, Captain Mikhail Pushkin had informed them that since both sons of the late Yuri Drakovich had commmitted no crimes on American soil they couldn't be extradited. Questioned about the strange events in Brighton Beach, yes, but not cuffed and whisked out of the motherland.

So be it. The Stony Man soldiers would do things the hard way. Bolan was fully armed with his standard sidearms. Grimaldi was likewise loaded and good to go. And in the trunk of the sedan was a mini-armory of everything the two would need to declare war on the Drakovich sons and army.

The only plus was the FSK Captain had given Bolan Vasily Smolenkov's address, and directions to his apartment.

As luck—or design—would have it, their two-hour surveillance of Smolenskov's Moscow apartment had paid off. If Bolan's new shopping list was accurate— and he had no doubt it was, coming direct from the Farm, during his update with Brognola while in the air—then Smolenskov was headed for a nightclub owned by both Drakovich sons. It didn't escape Bolan that the FSK captain could be dirty and have alerted their enemies to their arrival. Again experience warned him to expect as much.

"I read it just the way you do," Bolan told Grimaldi at length. "Which is why the upshot is we're working alone."

"With shadows."

"Always a possibility."

While surveying Smolenskov's apartment, Bolan had come up with a plan of attack, and he was ready to begin phase one. Brognola's only new information on the nuclear smuggling operations was that a number of Aeroflot employees, from baggage handlers to Customs people on up through two executives on the board of directors, had turned up dead in the past two days. No more mules had dropped in international airports. Bolan knew he and Grimaldi were completely on their own to root out answers.

The key to toppling the enemy, Bolan believed, was uncovering exactly where the nuclear goods were being shipped. The Farm was working around the clock to give Bolan something, anything, to point him toward what had to be the ultimate destination of their mission.

The Executioner watched the night. The limo pulled up in front of the Mafia's club. The new intel pack he had received in the air via fax told Bolan the place was called Drake's. It catered to the elite of Moscow who had money to burn. The soldier had seen this type of den before. Once inside he could expect to find a lot of Russian gangsters, their cronies and their women, with a smattering of legitimate businessmen who either found it fashionable or wanted to rub elbows with the local crime lords. Whatever he found inside he would take it as it showed. He would stick to plan, but if new cards were dealt his way he was ready.

Bolan saw a figure move from the front doors of the club, open the limo's back door. Smolenskov stepped out onto the sidewalk. The ex-KGB killer was quickly flanked by two hardmen, who also emerged from the vehicle. Grimaldi pulled over to the curb as Bolan watched several vehicles pass them. Ahead the soldier saw the Russian trio look around then disappear through the club doors. Two doormen watched the steady flow of patrons coming and going. Drakovich soldiers, no doubt. Getting past them might prove a problem, Bolan knew, if his description had been laid on the doormen from a justifiably paranoid Smolenskov or one of the sons. If he caught a minisurge going through the doors from either direction, Bolan figured he should be able to roll right in with the flow, unnoticed.

It was dicey, no matter what. Given what had happened in Brighton Beach, Bolan's suspicion was that a war council was under way. The troops would be on high alert, suspicious of any strange faces in the crowd, maybe trigger-happy and ready to prove their mettle to their bosses. A gun battle in the club was the last thing Bolan wanted, but he was prepared to go to the mat however it fell.

"Okay," Bolan told Grimaldi, "let me go shake some trees and see what falls out."

"If it goes to hell…"

"You'll be the first to know," Bolan told his friend.

One last look into the side-view mirror and he found only a smattering of traffic rolling their way. Then Bolan stepped out into the cold night air. Adrenaline, though, kept him warm, and the sidearms snug beneath his long overcoat gave him the only kind of comfort he needed.

And in his coat pocket the Executioner was bringing along a welcome-home gift for Vasily Smolenskov.

HE HAD TOSSED them the bone and they had bitten. The Americans were predictable.

Captain Mikhail Pushkin ordered his driver, Sergeant Zilaya Dodev, to pull into an alley directly across the street from Drake's but four blocks down then to kill the lights and engine. When that was done, Pushkin watched the tall American called Belasko roll into the nightclub. If he was going for low profile he succeeded, moving casually, not looking the doormen in the eye.

Something about this American disturbed Pushkin. He adjusted the weight on his 9 mm Makarov pistol in his shoulder holster beneath his coat, as if wanting to reassure himself the weapon was there. If matters got out of hand two AKM assault rifles were locked in the trunk, and he was grateful for the heavier firepower.

He sat in silence, giving the strange situation some thought. Pushkin hadn't survived the reshaping of the

KGB by being a stupid or careless man. No, when former comrades had retired from the KGB, Pushkin, looking ahead to his own future, had clung to important and powerful men who had moved on.

Generally speaking, moving on for the retired KGB officers and assassins Pushkin knew meant they were busy oiling the machinery of a criminal empire. In the early days, when the Drakovich crime family was just starting out, many had been called by Yuri Drakovich, but few in the FSK leaped at the opportunity to be the eyes and ears of what was to become the most powerful criminal organization in Russia. If they refused Drakovich's offer to be part of the Family, sooner or later they turned up with a bullet behind the ear.

He knew all too well the only thing certain in Russia was death and suffering. When his country had shed its armor of communism, Pushkin had quickly come to see that everything new in Russia was just the same as before, maybe even worse. Indeed only the strong survived. And the stronger were the ones with the most guns, the most money and the most vicious determination to take what they wanted. For all cries about the virtues of freedom for all, there were still widespread food shortages, rampant crime and corruption, sweeping unemployment, epidemic alcoholism, drug addiction and suicide among the masses. Not even the simplest of modern Western conveniences, such as plumbing and electricity, worked on a regular basis.

The new Russia was a nightmare.

No, it was better to live in the world of the Russian Mafia, to grow rich in the process of protecting and feeding them information about any movements against their operation. Far better, indeed, than never knowing when a shadow would rush up from behind and pump a bullet into his brain.

Pushkin started to feel depressed about having so easily become corrupted. Then he pushed what he knew were self-pitying thoughts out of his head because he knew he had a duty to fulfill, or else. What was done was done. Long ago he had begun accepting those fat monthly payments from an intermediary sent by Yuri Drakovich, and he was still looking forward to becoming a rich old man. Such was life in Russia.

But now the crime boss was dead, gunned down apparently by unknown assassins in his Brighton Beach restaurant. With the sudden death Pushkin worried if his life would change. News of Yuri Drakovich's death had reached him from Vlad Drakovich while he was en route for Moscow. In Pushkin's circle bad news always traveled fast, and everyone involved with the Drakovich Family needed to know the score. With the father dead, though, where did he stand with the sons?

Now he had these Americans, supposedly from the Justice Department, and his orders coming down from his superiors in the FSK to cooperate fully. His CIA liaison in Moscow was handing out what pretty much amounted to diplomatic immunity to these special agents. But Pushkin suspected something else was on the table. The Americans weren't there to simply question the Drakovich sons and Colonel Smolenskov. No, they didn't strike him as any special agents from the Justice Department, operatives from the CIA or any other legitimate American law enforcement agency. It was something cold and determined in their eyes, the way they moved, talked. Yes, he had seen their kind before, in the old KGB days when he had worked with wet teams. Worse, he suspected they had something to do with what had happened in Brighton Beach.

He watched the American watching the club, the one calling himself Jack Grisham. Right then Pushkin knew the Drakovich sons were in the back office of their club and that Smolenskov had been summoned to Drake's so they could further their agenda of nuclear smuggling.

Pushkin knew all about the Drakovich nuke operation. After all, the KGB had controlled and guarded the locations of all stockpiles of nuclear weapons, before and after many of the weapons were moved, supposedly for disarmament. Likewise they had officers stationed at most of the nuclear reactors in Russia. When the KGB formally ceased to exist sentry duties fell to the FSK.

It had been difficult at first, paying off the key people at nuclear-reactor facilities that were slated to be shut down because of economic woes. Again, if they didn't take money and kept their mouths shut they could take a bullet.

"Do you think you should try and call him again?"

Pushkin ignored Dodev for a moment, locked as he was in his worry and anxiety. "In a moment. I've left two messages already. I suspect they are in a very important meeting. I'll give them a little more time."

"And the Americans? What if they decide to disrupt the meeting, questioning the sons and Colonel Smolenskov? There could be serious trouble."

"It's why I led them here. As for serious trouble, it's what I'm counting on. A mere phone call may not convince the sons or Smolenskov. They may think I'm just being paranoid. But if these Americans are who I suspect, then the hands that feed us need to see them in the flesh.''

"May I ask, Comrade, if they aren't from the American Justice Department, just who you think they really are?''

Pushkin shook his head. "I don't know—yet. But I have this gut feeling we'll find out very soon.''

SMOLENSKOV MARCHED into the spacious back office, his newly hired guns on his heels. He found he had walked into the middle of intense squabbling between the two sons. With the death of their father jealous rivalry between these boys was the last thing he needed.

Smolenskov listened to the sons with growing impatience.

"Of course," Vlad growled, "the Americans will want to question us about the massacre in our father's restaurant. They may even come here, full of themselves, throwing around a lot of threats. You're the lawyer, you figure out how to deal with them. We can't be extradited, that much I know. They have no evidence that we committed crimes in their country.''

"I don't care about the Americans. I'll deal with them," Gregor said. "What concerns me is having our father's body returned safely here for a proper burial. You just stand there with his will telling me how you're in charge and hinting that I'm nothing more than some peasant. And that the operation must come to an immediate and satisfying close. Beyond our father's signature on those papers there's no proof they're even genuine.''

"Watch your tone, Gregor. I loved our father as

much as you, maybe more, and I'd never betray his trust.''

"What does that mean?"

"It means more than once I was out there on the streets risking my life, shedding my blood for the Family.''

Smolenskov tried to turn a deaf ear to what he viewed as petty backbiting. The long flight to Moscow had driven the ex-KGB to the point of murderous rage. Not to mention that the flight in the private Drakovich jet had been interrupted with an emergency call from one of their people in Brighton Beach. The Don was dead. It was really all any of them needed to know. It was time to pick up the pieces, find out who their enemies were and take care of the urgent business at hand.

Smolenskov decided it was time to take charge. "Enough!" The sons froze, startled. He read the resentment in their eyes as they stared at him. "Is this how you honor your father's memory? If he could see you now, standing there, squawking like peasants haggling over some meat pies. Act like men, like the soldiers your father would want. We have business to conclude and serious problems to address. Listen to me, both of you," he said, taking the edge out of his voice. "In a few days, after I have gone through a diplomatic channel open to me, I'll have your father's body flown back to Moscow for a proper burial. The American authorities will no doubt hold the body until they have spoken to you. I can take care of that matter. And, yes, as his friend, confidant and business partner I want nothing less than to see what happened to your father meet with the appropriate vengeance.'' He let that sink in, then nodded at the papers in Vlad's hand. "Now, let me see those papers."

The oldest son hesitated. He eyed the two soldiers then growled at Smolenskov, "Is it necessary we discuss personal business in front of others?"

Smolenskov clenched his jaw, fighting down his anger. He nodded at his two bodyguards, which told them to wait outside the door. When they were alone, Smolenskov marched straight to the desk and snatched the papers out of Vlad's hand.

The oldest son took offense at Smolenskov's rude gesture. "You may have been my father's closest comrade, you may have helped him create all we have, but I, Smolenskov," he said, his voice rising in anger, "am the sole inheritor of our ongoing business ventures. It states as much, in writing, and is signed by my father. And Gregor, not you, is my right hand. I expect you to acknowledge and honor that."

Smolenskov flashed both sons a strange smile. He flipped the papers back on the desktop. Yuri had typed out his will and signed it. It struck Smolenskov right then as strange how he knew their father better than they did, knew everything, in fact. There was no need for any of them to quibble or doubt the will. There was no need for anything other than the signature of Yuri Drakovich on the papers to verify their authenticity. His dead comrade always did things the old-fashioned way. Which meant a man did what he said he was going to do.

"I know all about what is in the will. Your father reviewed it with me when he wrote it."

Vlad stared at Smolenskov in angry disbelief. "What?"

"First, beyond you stating the obvious, that you two,

being his only sons, would inherit the kingdom, do you know what else is in there?'' Their hesitation and silence spoke volumes. ''But, of course. There are the names—in code—of the contacts and how and where they can be reached to further this present operation. Pick up those papers, Vlad, and turn to page three. If you aren't convinced I'll prove it to you.''

Smolenskov watched the confusion darken the oldest son's expression. ''You see that series of numbers?''

''Yes. And? What are they?''

''PALs.''

''What?'' Vlad growled.

''Permissive action links to a nuclear weapon.''

Now he had their full, undivided and very respectful attention.

''Yes, I see you understand. Allow me a moment. Our country—and because I am former KGB with the access, the security clearance to many facilities where nuclear weapons are stockpiled and know this for a fact—has a little over thirty thousand nuclear weapons.'' He shrugged. ''The Americans have been led to believe we only have twenty thousand.

''Anyway, when you were both mere children part of the duties of me and your father was to oversee several such facilities, and to assist in the shutting down of two designated nuclear power plants our then-Communist government could no longer afford to maintain. Of course a lot of radioactive waste had to be disposed of. As you know parts of our country are ecological disasters, Chernobyl being the one you and the rest of the world are most familiar with. There was a lot of what is called burned-up waste at one of these facilities, waste that we knew could be reprocessed into plutonium. We contracted mules to assist in the more hazardous areas. For instance, they were shown how waste could be repackaged into steel containers. We also had one light-water reactor dismantled, component parts secretly moved. Beyond the obvious and huge monetary gain that could be made from developing what I call Third World nukes, your father and I conceived a plan to save Mother Russia from a Western world we saw slowly attempting to strangle us and force us to become what we could never be.''

''Which is what?'' Gregor asked.

''One great nation under some faceless god of the masses, religion, one whining mass of a melting pot of all peoples, singing 'We are the World.' Freedom for everyone, money in everyone's pocket, the great dream of wealth. In reality, there can be no rich without any poor. Many must suffer so a few can live well. It's a simple law of nature. It's called survival of the fittest.

''Anyway, we used the contacts in the terrorist community. And, of course, these were the mules as you know. There's much more to the details of how the ones we hired were sent in to handle the uranium and plutonium, the waste, drill warheads to siphon out the plutonium…let's just say they were paid well and they were hungry to get their hands on what we promised them.

''I tell you—no, I warn you both. Look at and memorize those numbers on page three. Yes, yes, I know there are a lot of numbers to commit to memory. There's a good reason for that. They will activate an SS-20, a medium-range ballistic missile with three MIRVs, multiple and independent nuclear warheads weighing 150-300 kilotons. They can be fired from a tracked carrier, have a range of 4400 kilometers. The SS-20 itself is now sitting in a warehouse in Karachi, being guarded by our comrade there, Colonel Tuhbat. Why a renegade Pakistani colonel, accused of all manner of crimes, you ask? Very simple. The good colonel goes back many years with your father and me, assisted us in the pipeline of narcotics we opened. We have given him first dibs in the bidding war. Unfortunately without the PALs, ballistic data and operations manual, it's useless.''

He saw the sons studying page three, grim and intent.

''The colonel needs to come up with more money, however. But one SS-20 is only a small part of what your father and I set in motion. We didn't even really need those three mules who were killed during the attack on the warehouse. You see, what we have been sending out has already been processed. I know. I have already spoken to my two men in-country. The deal is set to go down.''

Clearly Vlad didn't like this new turn of events. ''My father seemed to have trusted you very much. I assume this isn't some game you're playing with us?''

''Implying?''

''Implying you'd rather have been the only one to inherit 'the kingdom' as you put it.''

Smolenskov choked down his rage. ''I'd watch your tongue, boy. If you don't proceed with this operation, if you think you two can sit back and rake in millions from other avenues, I'd read page five.''

Silently they read while Smolenskov said the words aloud. '''You will carry on the operation and even at the risk of your own lives. If you waver off the course of events I have set in motion, if you do not fulfill my obligations to our contracts Vasily Smolenskov will take over and make it happen.'" To make his point, he also recited the PALs. The sons looked impressed.

The colonel waited while they scoured the will. Finally they looked at him. "You act as if this is the first time you've both read it. What, you didn't bother to go past the part where you took over, Vlad? You didn't have your brother the lawyer read it?" Their angry silence told him the truth.

"I didn't have the time. Surely after all the events of the past two days you can understand. I've been busy trying to sort out the madness we find flung in our faces. I've been busy shoring up certain areas of our businesses here in Moscow and I have been forced to hire new soldiers to replace all the men we lost in New York."

"But, of course. Make the time now. Memorize those PALs, then burn that will. Don't look at me that way," he rasped when Vlad bared his teeth. "The very last words in that will state your father's insistence that you do just that."

Suddenly the cell phone on the desk rang. Vlad picked it up, punched on, said, *"Da."*

The first look Smolenskov saw on Vlad's face was confusion.

"What did you say?"

Vlad turned a look of cold fear on Smolenskov.

"Describe them."

Smolenskov felt his blood race. Something was terribly wrong.

"Stay on them and keep me informed. No, make no move, don't let them out of your sight."

When the oldest son slammed down the phone Smolenskov saw the same look of rage and madness he had seen on the face of their father, many times in the past.

"They're here."

"What did you say?" Smolenskov asked, unable to believe his ears.

The new boss roared, "Our mysterious hunters from America have arrived in Moscow. And the bastard who I'm sure murdered my father is sitting out there in my club!"

10

Bolan found the Mafia club loud, crowded and thick with smoke. He glanced around, right off spotting the goons in thousand-dollar suits. A quick head count showed ten in all, but it was hard to tell, with all the nooks and crannies, alcoves here, hallways there. Walking on, making sure he stuck close to moving patrons, Bolan avoided eye contact with soldier and patron alike.

The place was cavernous, all lights, gold and silver trimmings, black leather and teak, with two long bars on opposite sides of the sprawling dance floor. It wasn't hard to make the grim-faced watchers at various tables as gangsters. Meanwhile the roving hard force was strategically positioned around the club at all compass points. Bulges were visible beneath their coats. Each had wireless earpieces that warned the big American they could contact each other in an instant if trouble showed.

Waiting, the soldier again looked around casually. No sign of Smolenskov or the Drakovich sons. But he figured they had found refuge in a back office to discuss business.

The soldier had no idea how and when the enemy would move, but he grimly intended to make their business his business. At this stage, with the Don dead, he suspected they would pull out all the stops while not pulling punches. Part of Bolan's plan was to leave behind a message with the bartender that would further rattle the enemy, erode their confidence and strike fear deeper into their hearts. He wanted them running fast and scared. Bolan believed a nuclear feast was on the enemy's menu. It was simply a question of where and when.

Walking into the enemy's lair alone, with only the one-man backup, was a roll of the dice, he knew. They were outnumbered, and on hostile ground no less. Bolan saw no other option but to take the fight straight ahead and hope to get the enemy running into his gunsights.

But the main gist of the plan was to kidnap Smolenskov, both for Q and A, and as bait to get the sons scrambling. This new tactical approach wasn't in line with keep-it-simple but Bolan could feel time working against him.

The bartender finally acknowledged Bolan after a lengthy dialogue with two young women. He walked down the bar, eyeing the soldier with suspicion.

Bolan reached into his pocket, pulled out the black pouch and laid it on the bar. The bartender's suspicious look darkened when Bolan asked, "You speak English?"

He smiled as Bolan imagined a shark would. "But, of course. We are new Russia. I have many American comrades at Drake's."

Bolan nodded toward the pouch. "That's for Vasily Smolenskov."

"Who?"

"I don't have time for stupid questions, Comrade. Tell Vasily that's a gift from his American friend. I've come a long way to see he gets it. He'll understand. Well?''

The bartender hesitated, then said, "What do I get?"

To make sure the bartender was taken care of, Bolan peeled off a hundred-dollar bill, American, and held it out for him. "Listen, carefully, Comrade. I'll be talking to Vasily later. I know he's a busy man right now. But you'll see he gets my gift, right?"

The bartender plucked the bill from Bolan's hand, then nodded. "Yes, as good as done. Drink?"

"No. Have a nice night."

Bolan discovered he was making his retreat not a second too soon. He was looking around to see if any of the hard force might make a sudden play when he spotted Smolenskov bursting through a door at the far corner of the club. Bolan read the alarm on the Russian's face.

It had gone to hell. Smolenskov was aware his mysterious enemy was in the club.

All that mattered to Bolan right then was clearing out. Already Smolenskov, two goons and the Drakovich sons were elbowing their way through the crowd at the edge of the dance floor. Heart pounding, Bolan made haste for the door. Combat senses on overdrive, he was ready to free the .44 Magnum Desert Eagle and blast his way out if necessary.

The soldier hit the door and fell in behind a trio of suits making a loud and drunken exit. On their heels Bolan swept past the doormen, then began marching down the sidewalk. Glancing back the soldier saw the doorman giving the moving crowds around him an angry search.

ONCE THE SHOCK, terror and outrage had flooded out of him, Smolenskov steeled himself to deal with the crisis.

The mystery American shooter was in Moscow. He had walked right into the club, all balls, larger than life. Well, Smolenskov decided, he'd never leave the city alive.

Smolenskov shoved his way through the dancers, his wild eyes searching the club. If he saw the big American he would know him without a second look. He would never, *could* never forget those terrible eyes, piercing straight through his soul, all judgment, fire and steel. Flanked by the Drakovich sons, Smolenskov bulldozed women and men alike.

"Calm down," he heard Vlad snarling in his ear. He kept searching the club but the place was too big, too much flashing light and smoke, too many people. "I'm already on it."

Turning, Smolenskov found Vlad on the handheld radio, barking orders to his troops. Presumably the soldiers stationed outside the front doors were being alerted to the danger. Smolenskov kept moving toward the front doors, ears tuned for the sound of gunfire beyond the grating thunder of American rock and roll.

"Colonel Smolenskov! Sir!"

Wheeling, the ex-KGB saw the bartender by his side. The bartender held out a black pouch.

"What's that?"

"The bartender looked uncertain, as if he were the bearer of bad news and Smolenskov might shoot the messenger.

The colonel listened to the message. Something about his American comrade bringing him a gift. Teeth clenched, he grabbed the pouch and opened it. Before he delved into the bag he already suspected what he would find inside. When he pulled out the huge diamond he was surprised at his lack of anger. He hefted the diamond, muttered, "Oh, you bastard, I'll see your balls...."

He felt hands clawing into his shoulders. "One of the doormen thinks he spotted the American," Vlad told Smolenskov.

"Listen to me, Vlad, Gregor," he said, forced to shout above the loud music. "This operation demands we leave Moscow immediately. Put out a call to Suganov—he'll have every available soldier in the city looking for this bastard. Offer a substantial reward to the man who brings us the head of this American, offer even more if they can capture him alive. But we have no time to waste." He wasn't sure the sons were listening. "Do you hear me?"

"I want to see the murderer of our father die by my own hand!" Vlad roared. "Damn you, Smolenskov! Where is your loyalty?"

"Your father would want to see the completion of the operation. That's where my loyalty stands. He'd tell you to hold off on your vengeance until another day, that it will come in time. Let a force of hired guns deal with this American! I have an Antonov transport plane waiting outside the city. I made the arrangements from my apartment while I waited for you to contact me. We have a safe route to fly to Karachi, where we will meet the colonel. I suggest you go out the back door, both of you, get in your cars and meet me at the airfield. Do you know the one I'm talking about?"

"Yes. Where my father kept a private helicopter and another jet. Just south of Ogal."

"That's the one. Will you honor your father's will?"

It was what Smolenskov regarded as a moment of truth. The sons hesitated as they looked at each other.

"Well? Time is wasting."

"Very well," Vlad said.

"Gregor?"

"I will agree, for the moment. But I want to know the killer of our father is likewise dead. If I suspect you are being anything other than candid, Comrade..."

Smolenskov allowed the youngest son to let his threat hang in the air. "Fair enough. But your revenge, it will happen, somehow. Trust me on this. Go then," Smolenskov said, waited until they had spun on their heels to go out the back way. With his bodyguards flanking him, Smolenskov moved toward the front doors. He thought about his vehicle, and his heart began racing. If the bastard was out there waiting, it could seem like a mile until he reached the safety of his car. That, and a lifetime.

BOLAN FIGURED he had thrown it all to the wolves, then decided this sudden unlucky turn could work to their advantage. The enemy was now out in the open, and knew he was close.

Long strides carried him toward the parked sedan as he checked the street in both directions. Traffic was moderate, sidewalks packed with Muscovites, the mobs surging in and out of all the taverns, cafés and clubs in the neighborhood. He briefly wondered how much of this street belonged to the Drakovich Family.

Then he spotted the dark Zhigul, sitting in the mouth of an alley, two blocks down from their own car. The outer limits of light washed over the hood of the vehicle, and Bolan made out two shadows in the front. They were being watched.

As Bolan walked up on the driver's side, he told Grimaldi, "We've got a problem."

Grimaldi gave a knowing glance in the side-view mirror. "I see them, but I can't make out their faces."

"We've got more problems than just them. Give me the keys, I need to open the trunk."

Grimaldi said, "I can pop the trunk from here."

Good, Bolan thought, *keep the engine running.*

Moving quickly, Bolan lifted the trunk, hauled out a large canvas carryall that housed the heavy firepower.

Then he saw one of the doormen look his way, right in the eye, in fact. Smolenskov also spotted Bolan and shouted something to the doormen.

The colonel was piling into his waiting vehicle when one of his bodyguards joined the duo at the door. They cleared the crowd, and Bolan saw them digging into their jackets.

The soldier dropped the carryall and went for the Desert Eagle.

The trio of hardmen marched straight at Bolan. There was no crowd directly behind the enemy at the moment, and Bolan knew he would never get a better opportunity. He didn't want to risk the massive stopping power of the .44 Magnum slug drilling a target, continuing and hitting an innocent bystander.

The three were quick but Bolan was quicker.

And Grimaldi had seen them coming. He jumped into the act, out the door, with his Beretta drawn and tracking.

The Desert Eagle thundered in Bolan's double-fisted grip. He dropped the first hardman with a chest shot. The guy hit the pavement. The expected screaming and scrambling for cover of bystanders erupted next. Grimaldi caught another hardman with a head shot, but number three was crouching and pulling the trigger on his 9 mm Makarov pistol for all it was worth.

Somewhere between the gunfire and shouting, Bolan heard a squeal of rubber. He glimpsed Smolenskov's getaway as the ZIL swerved across the street and the driver gunned the engine, heading past the raging gun battle.

Bolan heard their vehicle taking hits, slugs drawing sparks off the roof. A bullet whispered past Bolan's ear, as he moved away from the enemy's tracking fire, heading for the cover of the pole of a street lamp.

PUSHKIN COULDN'T believe his eyes. One moment the tall American, Belasko, was saying something to Grisham, then the trunk popped open and, before he knew it, the Americans were engaging in a gun battle right on the sidewalk with Drakovich soldiers.

He heard Dodev curse, but there was nothing they could do but watch. Pushkin knew this sort of violence was commonplace in Moscow. There were roughly one hundred Mafia gangs in the city. All of them were vicious, greedy, trigger-happy and bloodthirsty. Every gang was looking to kill and extort their way up the pecking order. Rivalry and open warfare, including murder in full public view, kidnappings, even bombings happened all the time. The police were corrupted by Mafia money, and an investigation usually went no further than cleaning up the mess.

The Americans, Pushkin observed, were lightning-quick, had anticipated the threat and moved together like some well-oiled machine. One, then two Drakovich soldiers were nailed by gunfire. The third one had a chance.

But it was over in the next second.

Soldier number three absorbed a double punch of lead and appeared to fly in two directions for a split second, then did a hard pirouette and slammed to the sidewalk.

In the chaos of the crowd racing in all directions, Pushkin had forgotten all about his momentary sighting of Smolenskov. He had tipped off the presence of the American in the Mafia club, and he now believed himself to be the catalyst of this sudden violence.

And the gangsters, his employers, hadn't come out on top.

Smolenskov's ZIL roared past, and Pushkin watched it race down the street.

"What do we do?"

Pushkin heard the agitation and panic in Dodev's voice. He wasn't sure what to do himself, until he saw Belasko dropping into his vehicle. Grisham swung the sedan across the street, cutting off traffic coming in that direction. He was treated to a blare of horns and screech of rubber.

If nothing else, the gun battle just confirmed Pushkin's worst suspicions about the Americans. They were no U.S. Justice Department agents. No, they were in Moscow to kill Smolenskov and the surviving Drakovich sons. If they succeeded there would be a massive investigation by the authorities, which could lead in his direction, Pushkin decided. Not only that, but if the Americans killed his potential gold mine, it would take years, if ever, for Pushkin to groom another *Mafiya* source.

When Grisham blew the sedan past them, Pushkin growled, "Follow them. And be ready for anything."

Vlad Drakovich had been on the cell phone since evacuating his club. There were more disturbing developments, he had discovered. None of the news was good, and the thought danced through his mind at one point that he was cursed to fail his father. Perhaps the Drakovich Family had been on top for too long. The way to the top, where they had become the largest and most powerful criminal organization in Russia, was strewed with bitter enemies.

But a few shots of vodka had helped cement his resolve to carry on. He had to deal with the present crisis, which threatened to destroy them all. Not to mention the fact that he couldn't appear weak in front of his brother.

First he had called back the Family's FSK contact for a sit-rep. Pushkin informed him of the gun battle, of how Smolenskov sped away while three more of their soldiers were gunned down by the Americans. Drakovich had ordered his contact to keep tailing the Americans and to kill them the first chance he got. One way or another, he wanted them dead, and at this point he didn't care who did it. It would be a salve to his ego, a crowning achievement, of course, if they were captured alive, and he could kill them, slowly and in great pain, a trophy to hold up to any punk out there who thought he had lost the edge.

So, did Pushkin have any more to give him on these mysterious special agents of the Justice Department? No. But Pushkin told Drakovich of the CIA-FSK airfield north of Moscow, the FSK man believing that the Americans might eventually head back for their jet. Armed with that piece of information, Vlad Drakovich decided an ambush was in order.

The next call was to Ivan Suganov, the enforcer for the Drakovich Family in Moscow, just in case. A crew was ordered rounded up and Suganov was told what to do. He'd go to the airfield, where another FSK man would be on-site, paving the way for the hard force to kill the Americans, then move on with no one the wiser. A reward was offered for the Americans, dead or alive, but there could be a sweet bonus for Suganov if they were captured and brought to Drakovich, bloodied and begging for their lives.

The final call was to Smolenskov. The conversation had been extremely tense with Smolenskov informing him the Americans were right on his tail. The fear and anger in the man's voice rang loud and clear in Drakovich's ears. With only two armed soldiers to protect him, Drakovich knew Smolenskov was in serious trouble. Despite his suspicions about the Russian colonel's motivations, Vlad Drakovich knew he could ill afford to lose the man. Without Smolenskov's contacts the operation was in jeopardy of being either postponed, or hanging in limbo while their potential buyers wondered what the hell was going on. Of course, it could be done with or without Smolenskov. Even so, he had cajoled the necessary information out of the ex-KGB agent to track down Tuhbat in Karachi and even shore up the project beyond Pakistan. Since they were faced with an emergency situation and none of them knew how events in Moscow would fall, Smolenskov had provided him with key information to proceed. Apparently the bidding war was destined to take place in Yemen. That revelation made sense to Vlad, who knew the once-Communist South Yemen had been practically owned by the former KGB, and that his father and Smolenskov had spent a fair amount of time there training and arming terrorists.

Now Vlad Drakovich, sitting in the back of the ZIL limo, felt the angry silence hanging in the air between himself and his brother. Ignoring his brother's stare, he watched the flats, the drab apartment buildings that loomed around them as they made their way through the southern suburbs. A carload of soldiers was following their ZIL. Small comfort. He wondered if six men would be enough if the Americans suddenly appeared and started shooting.

And just who were these Americans? he wondered as he poured himself another shot of vodka. Certainly they weren't part of any legitimate, or sanctioned American law enforcement or intelligence agency. These men were proved hunters, killers of men, and they wouldn't rest until the entire Drakovich Family and all associates were wiped out. He decided who and what they were didn't really matter in the final analysis. What was important, as Smolenskov had pointed out, was honoring his father's will, ensuring the completion of the operation as declared, and even at the penalty of his own life.

He heard Gregor say, "Don't you find it suspicious that as soon as we arrive in Moscow these Americans show up? Killing our soldiers once again. And once again—and perhaps I'm stating the obvious—Smolenskov, our father's trusted comrade, is out there, on the run, giving us all this bad news? Do you actually trust Smolenskov?''

Vlad looked at his brother. He took the will from his coat pocket and held it up. ''We have no choice, Gregor. We have no say in the matter. As much as I don't like Smolenskov, he was with our father all these years. I'm forced into a situation I don't particularly care for, but I'll stay the course until we have succeeded in meeting our father's goals. Understand, Gregor, I'd like nothing more than for us to go back to normal business. The clubs, the restaurants, the black market small arms, the fencing of stolen jewelry, all the gambling, the whores and the drugs,'' he said, and saw his younger brother wince. Both of them knew, of course, how the Family fortune was made, but it was considered bad taste, even disrespectful, to mention the reality behind the wealth. Vlad wanted to make the point that he didn't care where the money came from as long as it kept coming. ''We're rich men because we have killed, corrupted, bribed and beaten the competition. Is it because you have become soft, Gregor, with no blood on your hands for some time now?''

''I'm in no mood to bicker with you.''

''Good. Then it's agreed, my brother, that we see this through, no matter what. No matter how bitter, how dangerous, how distasteful it may be.''

Gregor snorted. ''Distasteful? I tend to think of our current business more as madness. I know what this is all about, Vlad—I have for some time. We are making and selling nuclear weapons to fanatics.''

''And for more money in one day than we would make in five years from all our businesses combined.''

"Doesn't it bother you we could be the architects of the Third World War?"

No. As long as the missiles were detonated far away from Moscow, Vlad Drakovich didn't really care how many innocent people would be swept up in a mushroom cloud. Money was the only god he prayed to, pleasure the only altar before which he worshiped.

"What matters," he told his younger brother, "is that we're together in this to the end. Well?"

He watched Gregor carefully. Gregor looked away, and Vlad could almost feel his brother's conscience wanting to get the best of him.

"Gregor?"

"Do I have a choice?"

Vlad let the question hang for a long moment. "No. But neither of us has a choice. And that, my brother, is the hard truth."

BOLAN KNEW THEY WERE hemmed in, front to rear.

As Grimaldi maintained a thirty-meter-or-so distance from their target, the soldier observed the ZIL was making no evasive maneuvers, instead sticking to a smooth forty miles per hour.

No, they weren't looking to shake their tail, Bolan knew. He suspected Smolenskov was searching for an opportunity to waylay them for a quick and final riposte. It further deepened Bolan's suspicion that Pushkin was staying about three blocks or more behind. No flashing headlights from their FSK contact, or an attempt to drive up beside their vehicle to get them to pull over.

And Bolan had clearly seen the face of Pushkin sitting in his vehicle in the mouth of the alley when he and Grimaldi had gone off in pursuit of Smolenskov.

The FSK contact knew the deal, and he wasn't along for a tour of the city.

A good twenty minutes had passed since they left the killzone at Drake's. No other vehicles had fallen into the chase, if Bolan could even call it that. It was a plus that they only had five guns to deal with, but he stayed ready for the numbers to add up any moment.

Smolenskov's vehicle had been leading them on a southeast course, Bolan believed, toward the Moscow River. The ex-KGB killer had a plan and Bolan believed he would soon show it.

Grimaldi kept following the ZIL as it drove through the maze of streets. Ahead the soldier saw the lights of the city stretching across the river. A wide open area of no-man's-land yawned dead ahead, and the ZIL picked up speed as it raced through an open gate.

Grimaldi looked in the rearview mirror. "I've got that itch again, Sarge."

"They're going to try and scratch it for you. Somewhere in here. If my hunch is right they're going for a squeeze play."

Bolan had the Uzi submachine gun locked and loaded. He put the other Uzi SMG on the seat beside Grimaldi.

"That bastard Pushkin alerted Smolenskov. It makes me wonder just how dirty the FSK is."

"Just as well it turned out this way. We can't clean their whole house, and Hal knew it was risky when he dumped us in their lap. Now we know what we're dealing with. Pushkin will make a stand. He can't afford to let us keep on breathing now that we suspect he's on the Drakovich payroll. I counted two, three including Smolenskov."

"Have you considered the possibility Smolenskov may have called in the cavalry?"

"He's certainly had the time and he seems to know right where he's leading us. He knows the city, and even though we've been here before he could have easily ditched us, especially since he had a good two-minute head start while we were involved saving our skin."

"Yeah, and my reading of Cyrillic isn't up to snuff. I couldn't even tell you where we are."

"I want to take Smolenskov breathing, if possible. Leg shot, arm shot, whatever it takes. If we can't bag him alive this could be one colossal waste of time."

Indeed, at this stage, the soldiers knew they needed intel more than a higher body count.

Gunning the engine, Grimaldi cut the gap to the ZIL. They were rolling hard and fast between long rows of warehouses. The lighting was poor, in keeping with the end-of-the-world look and feel of the industrial wasteland. Bolan was juiced with combat senses, ready to greet whatever play the enemy made. It was going to happen, and soon.

The ZIL roared ahead on a sudden surge of power. The wheelman hit the brakes hard, throwing the vehicle into a hard slide, then slipped between another canyon of warehouses, where it vanished from sight for critical moments. It had been a lightning maneuver that only a pro could make, and it nearly caught Grimaldi by surprise. Even so, the pilot whiplashed the sedan into the plume of dust and trash in the ZIL's wake.

Dead ahead, Bolan discovered it was going to happen here and now. Smolenskov had given the order to make the grandstand play.

The ZIL's wheelman was hitting the brakes, throwing the vehicle around, nose first, so that the headlights speared right in the faces of the two soldiers.

"Bail out!" Bolan shouted, looking away from the glaring lights, hitting the door and clearing the sedan as two shadows emerged from the ZIL and opened up with autofire.

Uzi clutched tight in his fists, Bolan hit the ground hard. The air was punched from his lungs, but lack of oxygen quickly became his least worry. He was rolling fast and furious toward a Dumpster.

Poised to fire, the Executioner took in the battlefield in an eye blink. The two hardmen were spraying the sedan with gunfire. Obviously the enemy wasn't aware of the unmanned status of the sedan. Bolan suddenly glimpsed the tumbling figure of Grimaldi coming up on the opposite side before rolling for cover behind a forklift.

There was a lot of hollering and cursing downrange as the two hardmen tried to outrun the unmanned sedan. Just before the sedan bulldozed into the back of the ZIL Bolan glimpsed a third shadow diving from the vehicle.

Without hesitation, Bolan and Grimaldi went to grim work with their Uzis. Against the rending of metal and shattering glass, the two soldiers tracked the two hardmen with lethal precision as the Russians made a failing attempt to find cover.

The planned deathtrap had nearly snared Bolan and Grimaldi, but it was far from over, even as the combined stutter of Uzi autofire stitched the hardmen up their sides, spun them around so that 9 mm shots to the face kicked them off their feet.

In the periphery of a lone surviving headlight from the ZIL, as the sedan rolled on, Bolan made out the grim determination on Smolenskov's face. The ex-KGB killer was up and moving for a discarded AKM. It had all happened so fast, that Bolan had momentarily forgotten about Pushkin.

The Executioner saw the headlights washing over the no-man's-land between the warehouses, wheeled and saw the armed shadows leaping from the vehicle on his rear.

Bolan didn't have the time and certainly not the mercy to spare. Pushkin and Dodev burst out of their vehicle, tracking with assault rifles. There wasn't a word of warning, not a "Freeze, drop the weapons," from the FSK Agents. They began triggering their AKMs, slugs whining off metal above Bolan's head. But the Executioner and his friend beat them to it. Perhaps Pushkin and Dodev had believed the Americans would hesitate, not suspecting the real score. Bolan and Grimaldi proved them wrong.

A storm of 9 mm slugs chewed up the FSK men, blowing through the windows of the doors they stood behind, eating them up in sprays of blood and shredded cloth.

When they dropped, Bolan turned his attention on Smolenskov. The ex-KGB killer almost grabbed an AKM but Bolan blew the weapon out of the man's reach.

"Give it up, Smolenskov," Bolan said, slapping a fresh clip into his Uzi.

Smolenskov intended to go all the way, and the Executioner gave the man credit for resolve. Grimaldi followed Bolan's play, blasting the AKM out of the ex-KGB killer's grasp just as his fingers touched the weapon.

Running, Bolan made Smolenskov as he tried one last desperate attempt.

The Executioner buried a foot deep into Smolenskov's stomach. As he belched air, squirmed and sucked wind, the soldier patted Smolenskov down for any hidden weapons. Satisfied with the search, Bolan pulled a pair of handcuffs from his coat pocket. He pinned the Russian to the ground with a knee to the neck and slapped the cuffs on his prisoner.

The Executioner found Grimaldi fanning no-man's-land with his weapon. Nothing moved in the shadows around them, no sound other than Smolenskov's bitter cursing.

It was time to go. Roughly Bolan hauled Smolenskov to his feet.

12

Ivan Suganov believed the fate of an empire had been dropped on his shoulders.

Since the call from Vlad Drakovich, then the roundup of his crew, on through the drive to this CIA-FSK airfield, Suganov felt the juices, his lust to kill, burn like fire in his blood. If he pulled off this hit it would be his crowning achievement. Indeed, there would be a ripple effect of fear and respect through not only the Drakovich organization, but all the Mafia Families in Moscow. They would know and speak the name of Ivan Suganov with the awe and respect he felt was his due. Ten years of killing in the shadows for the Drakoviches. And for what? No glory, no hefty hike in pay. Oh, maybe a glass of vodka raised to him, a hearty "well done" from the Boss in front of the troops, or maybe an envelope with a bonus tucked into his coat pocket.

How many men—and women—had he killed for the late Yuri Drakovich? Add up all the soldiers from other Mafia families, or police informants, he thought, maybe a businessman here and there who didn't think he should cough up payments to the Family for protection, and he figured he was in the neighborhood of over two hundred kills.

But so much for past victories. That was then, and this night was make or break, do or die.

The time had come to earn the right to his crown.

No sooner did the two ZILs roll to a stop, than the main gate was rolling wide. Grabbing his AKM, Suganov slid out of his vehicle, watching his twelve-man crew emerge from the ZILs, all of them grim as hell, hard and sharp as the steel of a bayonet. With all the AK-47s, Dragunov sniper rifles and RPG-7 rocket launchers hauled from the trunks they could start and win a small war. The hardware should be more than enough to take down two men, no matter how good the opposition.

Suganov had handpicked each man for the job. They were the best that money could buy, and they had proved their mettle more often than there had been revolutions and the changing of czars in the history of the motherland.

If the Americans were as good as he expected—no, hoped, well, a thirteen-way split was a stretch. The payday he craved was one that would land him that nightclub he had always dreamed about. Smoking cigars, drinking bottomless vats of vodka, having women in the prayer position before him, his own crew of soldiers....

A man could dream, couldn't he? But his dreams were on hold, at least until he saw the two Americans dead at his feet, and there was cash in hand. Time to pull it together.

A lone figure in the green uniform of the FSK, armed with an AK-47, stepped from the guard booth.

Suganov moved to meet his prearranged FSK contact. He already had some of the preliminaries, but he needed more facts.

"Comrade Ptomkin?"

Suganov rolled his massive bulk up to the FSK agent, towering over the man. Muscles bulged beneath Suganov's black leather trench coat and his shoulder-length black hair was tied back in a ponytail.

"*Da.*"

Suganov gave his surroundings a long search, assessing points of attack, his mind clicking into strategy, killer instincts flaring to life. Woods flanked the airfield, if he could even call it that. There was only one runway, east to west, tarmacs, several choppers grounded in the far southwest corner. Three hangars at a southwest point, roughly a thousand meters away. There was a control tower to the north that would make a nice platform to position a fire team. A searchlight could be manned to throw down a blinding light at the appropriate moment. Further inspection revealed the airfield was hemmed in by a chain-link fence topped with razor wire. To the south, he heard a jumbo jet thundering to takeoff from Sheremetyevo International. All in all, he decided this was a clean and simple enough setup for what he had in mind, and the shriek of jets coming and going would drown the noise of gunfire.

"Report," Suganov ordered.

"Everything is in order. The CIA agents stationed here were called away by an FSK man on a tip that their embassy may be the target of a terrorist attack. They'll be gone for hours."

They had the run of the place, and that was the good news. Eventually Suganov expected the CIA men to return, but hopefully only after he was long gone, flush with success.

"The Americans have been gone for nearly twenty

hours. I haven't heard from Captain Pushkin. I'm concerned.

"Assume the worst. Their jet?"

"In the middle hangar, but as I explained, they have a magnetic card, the only method by which to open the hangar doors. There's no way to bypass it, and if it's forced open the CIA will be alerted through an alarm system at the American embassy."

Suganov shook his head in disgust. "The CIA and former KGB working together. What has the world come to? Well, at least it's good to see neither side still completely trusts the other."

Small comfort.

So sabotaging the jet was out, Suganov knew. Of course, he could always blow the door down to disable the jet, but a gaping hole in the hangar would only alert the targets. Never mind. The only way the Americans would fly out would be in body bags.

Mentally he laid out the ambush, figuring three separate points of attack with interlocking fields of fire. He scanned the runway and spotted a dip in the land just to the south of the runway lights. While Suganov envisioned his master plan, he heard the FSK man prattle on about no air traffic being expected until the morning. Suganov, keeping a tight leash on the beast inside him, heard the basics he already knew. Dark sedan, CIA vehicle, no armor-plating, reinforced glass. He wasn't sure what the Americans were armed with or when they would return.

Enough.

Suganov took the fat brown envelope from his coat pocket and handed it to Ptomkin, who opened it and examined its contents, giving the Mafia hitter a blessed moment of silence.

"Count it later. Is the uniform I asked for inside?"

"Yes. Will that be all?"

"Clear out."

While he waited for the FSK man to go to his vehicle and depart, Suganov barked out orders all around. He had the brief wrapped up in sixty seconds. They knew what to do, and what was expected of them.

If they couldn't do the job then nobody could, and Vlad Drakovich would be hung out there with a future not even worth considering.

GIVEN WHAT he knew so far Bolan didn't find Smolenskov's version of events and of the history of the muling too far from the truth. The more Smolenskov talked, the more a few of the pieces, though still jagged, began to fit.

They were rolling north through Moscow with Grimaldi at the wheel. Their sedan was a little worse for wear. The front headlight was gone and the fender on the passenger side was smashed in from the collision with the ZIL. Before leaving the warehouse grounds, both men had pored over a map of the city, outlined the quickest route to Dmitrov Highway. From there it was straight to the airfield. If the alert and their descriptions had gone out to the police, they could find themselves faced with the problem of a roadblock. Bolan was counting on their quick escape from the city.

Even so it was all too easy, and Bolan never trusted easy. Some obstacles with weapons aimed their way would rear up at some point. But Bolan was ready to fight his way out of Russia, if necessary. He could be sure his friend was locked into the same mind-set.

Knowing his paranoia and suspicions might prove justified, the soldier had hauled out M-16/M-203 combos, one each for the Stony Man duo. Before rolling from the warehouse killzone Bolan and Grimaldi had put on combat harness, with three frag grenades each and spare clips for their sidearms and main assault piece.

Smolenskov's willingness to talk about the operation, or, rather, throw out bits and snatches, was just enough to keep Bolan guessing or appeased. After the soldier had positioned himself in the back seat with the Russian and made sure the cuffs were tight, he told the ex-KGB man, "We need to talk about the nuclear smuggling. This is a one-time offer. And you've seen we're on a tight schedule." No gun drawn, no backhand to the face necessary, Smolenskov calmly launched into facts, figures and details. Simple as that. Too simple. Bolan wasn't about to fool himself. A crew of hitters, more than likely, had been rounded up by the enemy, sent out into the streets to hunt down and kill them. Smolenskov was most likely buying time.

To make sure they weren't blindsided, Grimaldi kept vigilance on their surroundings as they rolled on, between the flats and apartment buildings on the northern outskirts of Moscow.

While Smolenskov took a break in his monologue, Bolan gave the dark streets a quick search. Light traffic, but the sidewalks were packed with shadowy throngs in search of whatever it was that got them through the night. To the east, as they crossed a main avenue, the soldier caught a glimpse of the glowing spires marking Red Square, the onion dome of St. Basil's Cathedral rising into a skyline that looked misted by the glare of red lights.

He turned grim attention back to Smolenskov. Bolan wasn't sure what to believe, but was pretty certain

Smolenskov was blowing out enough smoke to keep dancing around the tough questions.

"So, you're telling me," Bolan said, "for twenty-five years you and Drakovich and a handful of others have been hard at it, dismantling reactors, siphoning out radioactive waste, shipping off component parts to build a reprocessing plant, without anyone, least of all the CIA, catching on?"

"I have no reason to lie. You have the gun."

"The way I'm reading it, you're lying by omission."

"Perhaps you need to learn how to read better."

"You don't wear sarcasm well, Comrade. Fill in the blanks or I'll lose patience. In this case, losing patience means I get trigger-happy."

Smolenskov stared deep into the fire in Bolan's eyes, but the soldier wasn't sure he'd made the man a believer.

"Surely I needn't tell you that the KGB ran Russia. Before it's transformation into its present sorry state of ineptitude and corruption, the KGB was the most powerful and privileged institution in Russia. We had access to all nuclear stockpiles, the PALs to all missiles. We were the overseers of several nuclear reactors. More than a hundred thousand ex-KGB officers have the necessary codes to all manner of nuclear weapons, including ICBMs. We can make a dozen SS-20s vanish into thin air, if we want."

There was something in that statement, the way Smolenskov said it, the look in his eyes, proud and defiant, that drove an icy chill down Bolan's spine. He would get back to the vanishing SS-20s remark soon.

"Is it so hard for you to believe that we could smuggle out any manner of nuclear weapons, or the necessary material to build one? Even if we had to scrape the bottom of the plutonium barrel?''

Bolan knew what Smolenskov said was all too horribly real. ''You weren't looking to fire up some Third World country's cities as the sole provider of electricity, so I'm convinced on that score. I'm having some trouble with your version of who's involved and how you managed to keep it hidden for so long. First of all, even after a reactor is shut down, you've got radioactive fission in fuel rods and the core reactor. Everything is simply too hot to handle for a long time. Dismantling a reactor takes time, technical expertise. Even with protective suits, you've got the problem of constant decontamination and the disposal of tons of radioactive waste.'' He recalled some more of the facts Stony Man Farm had put to him, just to let Smolenskov know he knew a part of the deal. ''With a few mules flying around, it would take years to smuggle the necessary fuel rods, just for starters. When they were cut open after dying on planes and in terminals, a couple of them were found to be swallowers of uranium pellets. Figure the math—two hundred pellets to fill a twelve-foot rod, each pellet with the same amount of energy as a ton of coal. You need a hundred tons of pellets alone to fire up a reactor.''

Anger flashed through Smolenskov's eyes. ''It was done. Perhaps the how isn't even so important anymore.''

''I'll grant you that. Okay, I'm waiting to hear more, Smolenskov, something you can give me that might keep you breathing.''

''Okay. The muling. I was against the muling, the bringing in of the terrorist contacts we had accumulated over the years. When they were exposed to radioactivity, I knew it was only a matter of time before they fell ill and eventually died. Yuri Drakovich was in a hurry to complete his goal, to see it succeed after waiting and struggling for so many years. When they fell sick we put money in their pockets, shipped them off to some country to lay low with promises of medical attention and that their sickness would pass."

The guy was dancing, repeating himself, but Bolan played the game, content to hand Smolenskov a little more rope for the moment. "Like the Saudi prince's buddies who turned up dead in Somalia?"

That threw Smolenskov off for a moment. But the man pulled himself together, scrambling to organize a response. He nodded. "Precisely. I would have preferred executing them outright and disposing of the bodies."

"Very considerate of you."

"Considering how they died, I thought so. Besides, word may have reached our other mules that we thought they were expendable."

"You didn't want dissension in the ranks. And they were expendable."

"It was sloppy, having them repackage the radioactive material, I warned Yuri."

"Even sloppier to use Aeroflot. Why not just use a private transport plane or a ship?"

"Yuri used the airline to move a lot of drugs from the east. He had many connections in Aeroflot. If we used private transport as you stated, well, getting through Russian airspace without a logged flight plan could prove disastrous. However, the bulk of the component parts, a lot of fissionable material was moved by private transport, using airspace and travel routes reserved for KGB VIPs only. He laid out a program where he could continually use mules, an elaborate system where pellets, rods, U-238 could always be moving. Around the clock.''

''So, when your mules started dying off you realized the whole conspiracy was set to come unraveled.''

Bolan was probing easy, but spotted the shadows behind Smolenskov's eyes, all the telltale signs the ex-KGB man was hiding something.

''I get the feeling you're stalling, Smolenskov.'' It was time to play hardball. Bolan pulled out the .44 Magnum Desert Eagle and watched the fear flicker through Smolenskov's eyes. ''Answer my question. Where?''

Smolenskov wanted to get defiant, the soldier saw, lapsing deeper into brooding silence. Without warning, Bolan clubbed Smolenskov over the head with the big gun's barrel. The former KGB killer grunted, cursed and felt the blood trickling down the side of his head.

''That was a love tap. Next time...'' he said, letting the sentence drop.

Bolan could almost see the wheels spinning as Smolenskov looked away, teeth clenched, fire in his eyes. Finally he nodded several times, a gesture that told Bolan that where the man still had life there was hope.

''Okay, okay. Not that it matters. Not that you might live to see the next sunrise. Yemen. Or, what used to be South Yemen, Communist Yemen.''

Finally they were down to business. Even so, he was far from the hard truth, Bolan sensed. But like the blood running from the gash in Smolenskov's head, the Executioner knew the facts were going to leak out one way or another.

13

Gregor Drakovich believed he could sense when events were spiraling out of control, when some awful fate was waiting at the end of the line.

Oh, he had killed on more than one occasion, but never the cold-blooded executions, those sudden storm killings of well-armed and determined rivals that had made his older brother a force to be feared. On the flip side of that sort of laser-focused brutality, Gregor Drakovich had killed but only in self-defense, always some rival soldier from another Family gunning for him. On those rare occasions when he had been called to arms, it was simple luck more than skill, spotting an onrushing or lurking adversary, shooting first, no questions.

Forget memory lane, he chided himself. He had serious problems to tackle in the present, with a future shadowed by doubt and fear. He clung to images of himself as a warrior just the same.

In light of the Brighton Beach tragedy, with their mystery American hunters dogging them relentlessly and what he feared lay ahead, the younger brother suspected that whatever martial skills he owned would soon be tested.

So Gregor Drakovich stood in the belly of the giant Antonov transport plane, watching his older brother hurling out the weapons all around to the twenty-man force he had hired on the fly. In his private and troubled moment, he had to admit he respected Vlad, even liked and admired his older brother for his take-charge way. Vlad always commanded respect, always made it work, with no questions asked by the troops. That Vlad was bulling ahead with the sketchy framework their father had left behind to conclude some mega-nuke deal no longer troubled Gregor. His brother was simply playing true to character, and was hell-bent on seeing the dream become reality.

For a moment, Gregor could almost see their father smiling from the grave. If nothing else he would honor his father's will, even if he didn't like being relegated to something of the role of a flunky.

He tried to shake dark thoughts from his head. He felt the sweat break out beneath the khakis he had changed into on his brother's order. No silk threads, no patent leather shoes. It was fight time, according to his brother.

Pakistan and a lone SS-20 in question were on the table.

Still no word from Smolenskov. Vlad had been trying like hell to raise the man for the past hour or so. And there lay more uncertainty, their backs exposed even more, many questions he had about Smolenskov, the man's motivations, character. They were flying off, with or without Smolenskov, either way. Vlad had said as much. For a fleeting moment he was surprised to find a part of him hoped Smolenskov, a man he never liked or trusted, had met some bad fate.

Such as the two Americans.

If nothing else, Smolenskov's demise would lay to rest any question of a power struggle between the sons and the former KGB man.

He waited, while Vlad scanned the will and began punching in numbers on the computer keyboard next to the radio console. Gregor turned away, shaking his head to himself over his brother's stubborn refusal to see reality.

There were too many people, bad people, all over the map who knew too much about the operation. Everyone from the Pakistani colonel to the Somali warlord, the junkie Saudi prince on up to the powers-that-be in the Yemeni government and military. Greed motivated men to do things, he thought, they wouldn't normally do. Like bite off the hand that fed. Like kill without blinking, grab up what they could and run. The astronomical amount of money the Family was asking for in the bidding war would never be brought to the table. It was too much money, and his father's own greed, he feared, would cause them grief in time. The kind of trouble, he believed, that meant they would never set foot on Russian soil again.

Try telling Vlad.

Lost in some black hole deep inside, Gergor wasn't aware of his brother's presence beside him until Vlad grabbed his shoulder.

"What's the matter with you? I'm talking to you."

Slowly Gregor turned and looked his brother in the eye. And he didn't like what he saw. There was madness in his brother's eyes, and Gregor felt the fear slicing through him.

"I have contacted our men in Karachi. It seems the numbers correspond from the will."

"Was there ever any doubt?"

"No, at least not on my part. At any rate, a Mujwhal and an associate of our father's, Viktor Dtechka, will be awaiting our arrival. I have the flight plan here.

They laid it all out for our pilots, the safest route to avoid radar detection while flying across the border. However," Vlad said grimly, "they told me there is a problem. Exactly what, they wouldn't say until we arrive at the designated airfield."

Only one problem? Gregor Drakovich thought. Their problems had begun in Brighton Beach, two problems, in fact, who were at that very moment looking to reach out and annihilate them. Whoever their mystery hunters were, he knew they wouldn't rest until both sons were dead. It was the only thing he could be sure of.

Gregor watched as Vlad hauled a mini-Uzi from a crate. Without warning he tossed the weapon and Gregor caught it.

"Do you know how to use that weapon?"

He didn't, and told Vlad as much.

"I'll see that you get a quick lesson."

Alone, he watched as his older brother, the new boss, went off, again looking over the will. The words of their dead father seemed to fuel Vlad with an even more merciless determination, no, a hellish sort of angry drive, he decided.

That will, Gregor Drakovich feared, would lead them to their ultimate destiny. He only hoped the orders of a dead man didn't run them straight to their own damnation.

AGAIN SMOLENSKOV gave it up too easy for Bolan's liking. The soldier mentally digested their prisoner's data while Grimaldi forged ahead, rolling due north on the highway leading to the airfield. Both soldiers frequently checked behind and in front of them. So far smooth sailing. Too smooth, nagging Bolan that something was soon to go wrong.

According to Smolenskov the reprocessing site was roughly a hundred klicks due north of Aden. The story went that a Russian company, Vladovich, had sent a team of petro experts to South Yemen a good two decades ago. Drilling equipment was flown in by cargo planes. The proper Yemeni powers-that-be had long since been briefed and greased to look the other way. Vladovich was a KGB-owned company that supposedly handled industrial machinery, and it was run by the late Yuri Drakovich. Under the guise of oil exploration and drilling the component parts for a nuclear reactor, and the technicians and scientists to put it together were flown to this site. Around-the-clock dynamite blasting in the hills on a surrounding desert wasteland, and the plant was erected below ground by a small army of Russian and Yemeni laborers. Both Russia and Yemen eagerly used the other to attain the goal of building the bomb, the Yemenis with dreams of becoming a nuclear power, the Russians with sights set on a gold and silver rainbow of obscene cash profit.

At any rate, Bolan would have the Farm scan the area in question with satellite recon. If there was radioactivity in the area it would show up.

Again Bolan sensed Smolenskov's eager tongue was wagging over some critical detail. It was a long shot, but Bolan decided a bluff was in order, as a vision of an SS-20 came to mind.

"You mentioned earlier something about the KGB being able to make an SS-20 disappear."

Smolenskov kept a straight face, but his eyes narrowed just enough to warn Bolan he was on to something. "I did?"

"A dozen to be exact. I've got a couple of Pakistanis

who were muling for you, dead on arrival a while back.''

"Is there a question in my near future?"

"First, I believe you don't even need the mules any longer. I think you've already put together one or several missiles. It, or they, is up for sale. And I think if you were going to use the mules again, you'd go private transport. But only because you're on the verge of success and you can continue to build nuclear weapons in the future from this reprocessing plant. How am I doing so far?"

Smolenskov shrugged, and Bolan continued. "Right now, you've got a bidding war lined up, and my guess is it's either in Pakistan or Yemen. It's a game of who has the most ready cash. A Saudi prince, a Somali warlord, maybe another terrorist group with money to burn."

Smolenskov pursed his lips, nodded, seeming amused. "You have a very active imagination. Interesting."

"Interesting isn't what I'd call it."

"What would you call it then?"

"Greed and utter madness." Bolan paused, watching Smolenskov's face maintain a blank expression. The flickering of eyes, though, betrayed the Russian. Without warning Bolan went to the hard approach. Before Smolenskov could blink the Executioner shoved the .44 Magnum Desert Eagle under the man's chin, forcing his head up and back. Bolan's look, voice were all ice, as he said, "The SS-20s you mentioned. Where are they?"

Smolenskov swallowed hard. "Again, not that you will live to see..."

"The SS-20s."

"Karachi. And there is only one. Myself and the Drakovich boys were on our way to collect the money from a Colonel Atta Tuhbat. It's sitting in a warehouse."

Bolan was hardly uplifted by the revelation, but he had what he needed to move on to the next phase. Still, it was a worst-case scenario, however it was sliced. An SS-20 in the hands of someone able and willing to use it, he knew, could wipe out an entire city.

"Your Pakistani comrade has the missile, but you've got the PALs?" Bolan asked. Smolenskov's silence spoke volumes.

Pulling the gun away, the Executioner met Grimaldi's grim face in the rearview mirror.

"We need to phone home ASAP. We've got our work cut out for us."

"The understatement of the millennium. First things first," Bolan said.

"This ride's been too smooth. I keep waiting for the proverbial feces to hit the fan."

Bolan looked at Smolenskov. Again instinct moved the soldier to ask the Russian something else. "Drakovich has a hit team looking for us, doesn't he? Your boy Pushkin told him about the airfield. I'm thinking there's a crew waiting for us at the end of the line."

Smolenskov looked like a man walking to the gallows. "And if there is?"

The soldier let it ride. The silence thickened with tension and prebattle nerves. Waiting for it to happen was the worst part. Once they were in the middle of the action Bolan knew skill, experience and old-fashioned guts would get it right for the visiting team. Then again, they might just drive straight to their hangar, fly out, no sweat.

Bolan almost laughed out loud over that wishful thinking.

"Let me ask you something," Smolenskov said.

Bolan was treated to a mix of anger and curiosity from the prisoner.

"I have been the mouse all along, the bloody chum to the shark, if you will. It has been most unpleasant, to say the least. You took my diamonds, yet I sense you're not in this for the money."

Smolenskov paused and released a heavy, troubled breath, and Bolan said, "I'm listening."

"What then? Do you want the SS-20 and what we have produced in Yemen for yourself?"

"No."

"Then why? I'm most curious. With your obvious skills, this relentless determination of you two to destroy our organization, you could have been one of us. You could have been rich men beyond your wildest fantasies."

"I have my own vision. And a desire."

Smolenskov looked baffled as hell as he scoured Bolan's face. "Of what? For what?"

"Hope."

"For what?"

"A better tomorrow."

"KILL THE LIGHTS. Stop here."

Grimaldi doused the headlights, then braked.

It felt wrong to Bolan. It was too still, too silent, too dark out there on the airfield.

They were stopped on the road that led to the main gate, maybe fifty yards from the guardhouse.

Someone should have come out to meet them.

It was going to happen here, no doubt about it, Bolan sensed.

The soldier took the high-powered infrared binoculars from his carryall. A quick search of an area off the runway, to the south, showed four gray-green specters, stretched out prone near the runway, weapons ready. As he scanned on, the heads of three more ghostly shapes came to view, perched on the darkened platform of the control tower.

It took some adjusting of the lens, but the soldier focused in on their hangar. A thousand meters or so away, he zeroed in on a lone shape, again in the prone position, perched atop their hangar. Under any other circumstances, Bolan would have smiled in appreciation, given due respect. It was the perfect setup for an ambush.

"We've got a welcoming committee," Bolan told Grimaldi.

Less than thirty seconds later, they had the drill down, at least in theory, numbers that Bolan had a fix on, positions, and how to proceed.

The soldier used the butt of his M-16 and smashed out the overhead light. With his M-16/M-203 in hand, the M-203's breech loaded with a 40 mm shell for their ambushers, Bolan hopped out the door. He heard Grimaldi hitting a button to lock their prisoner in. Smolenskov was about to go for the ride of his life.

There was no other way, no choice but to make a hard run for the hangar, give it all they had. Staying put wasn't an option, nor was a long taxi in their jet down the runway under enemy fire.

The Executioner made haste for the edge of the tree line that ran up the side of the main road. He was moving ahead when Grimaldi put the sedan into drive.

The Stony wheelman put the pedal to the metal. There was a squeal of rubber as tires grabbed at asphalt, then the vehicle became a battering ram as it charged the main gate.

As he knew they would, Bolan found things turned ugly in a hurry.

Two shadows rolled up behind the main gate and cut loose on the sedan with blazing AK-47 automatic fire.

14

No sooner had he put the sedan into drive, leaving plenty of room to roll up a head of steam, than Grimaldi saw the enemy emerge from behind the guard booth.

There was no clear fix on enemy numbers or all possible points of attack, no way to know if the hangar, or even their jet was boobytrapped. At any rate, the Stony Man pilot had all the confidence in the world Bolan could score a clean sweep to the rear and flanks while he paved the charge. All Grimaldi had to do was crash the gate, blow past the two shadows with AK-47s and make a hard thousand-meter charge through a gauntlet of gunmen winging bullets and God only knew what else at him to get to the hangar.

Then Smolenskov decided to add to Grimaldi's problems. As the pilot floored the gas pedal, and the vehicle surged ahead, the shadows opened up with autofire. Smolenskov began roaring out a string of obscenities. It was a sudden spectacle that distracted Grimaldi for a critical second. The gunmen ahead were scoring hits on the windshield, a line of spider-webbed holes punching through the glass. Grimaldi ducked the hail of lead, glass slashing at his face, as the windshield gave way in jagged chunks to the blistering storm of heavy gunfire. He went through the gate, wind and

glass slapping at his face. Smolenskov was shouting
and thrashing around, kicking the driver's seat like a
man possessed.

Teeth gritted, his backside drilled by Smolenskov's
venting of either fear or retaliation, Grimaldi swerved
the vehicle on a hard course southwest, as the plan
called for. It was sheer brutal intent on the pilot's part
that he bowled through one of the gunmen attempting
a last-second bolt out of the path of his rampage. A
heavy thud and a sharp cry of agony, then a glimpse
of a dark figure sailing away, and Grimaldi discovered
things were just getting heated up.

From the south and north weapons fire erupted. The
enemy was making an all-out floor show of catching
the sedan in interlocking fields of fire.

Suddenly a harsh beam of light flared to life from
the control tower. Following the light, Grimaldi spotted
several muzzle-flashes illuminating the platform from
that direction. How many gunmen had him sighted and
were tracking?

The searchlight nearly pinned him down as bullets
hammered the hood and roof and the passenger window was shot out beside him in a sudden eruption of
glass. But he was racing ahead, veering hard off the
runway, out of the search beam. The engine revved like
thunder, tires clawing at soft grass as Grimaldi maneu-
vered the vehicle around, getting the second prong
of the ambush lined up for head-on bulldozing.
Smolenksov had gone berserk, pummeling the door behind Grimaldi with his feet and screaming profanities
at the top of his lungs even as the back window was
blasted out by tracking autofire from the rear.

Flying along at sixty mph and rising, the searchlight
bouncing around him, Grimaldi made out three, then

four gunmen rise up and cut loose with AK-47s. Ahead and closing fast the hard force was firing away as if there were no tomorrow, muzzle-flashes lighting the gloom. Then two figures began to shuffle around as the sedan rocketed straight at them. Grimaldi was locked in.

From some point directly above, a jumbo jet thundered low over the battlefield, the dark behemoth sweeping into Grimaldi's sight for a heartbeat, as if the pilot, copilot and passengers were looking for ringside seats.

Bullets spanged off the hood, ricocheted, then slashed jagged teeth off what remained of the windshield. Grimaldi flinched, ducked low behind the wheel. Twenty meters and closing on the gunmen, who decided in a sudden show of brazenness to hold their ground.

It was a fatal error in judgment for two of them. A fast reload of their AK-47s, though, and they went back to full-auto hosing. Eyelids slitted against the wind and flying glass slivers, the pilot aimed the sedan right at the muzzle-flashes that seemed to be leaping at his face from mere inches away.

Then the earth blossomed into a fireball behind the sedan. The heat of the blast reached out and blew through the vehicle. Rocket fire, Grimaldi knew, probably coming from the control tower.

Riding the thunder of the explosion, Grimaldi bulldozed through the second prong. He scored two hits, as flesh yielded to metal with wet-sounding thuds and the distinct snapping of bones before the bodies were hurtled off into the night.

The searchlight had the pilot locked in for a moment. His heart raced even more, then there was sudden and blessed darkness. Now what? Rolling on, Grimaldi began swerving the vehicle from side to side in a desperate defensive maneuver meant to throw off the enemy's aim. The hangar was within sight, and closing, putting him well within range of whatever the lone shadow on the roof was armed with.

Hardly the homestretch.

There was another explosion at Grimaldi's rear, but it was more like the sound of distant rolling thunder this time. A glance into the passenger side-view mirror and Grimaldi saw the control tower go up in fire and smoke. Bolan was hard at work.

It suddenly struck Grimaldi that it was very quiet in the vehicle. He didn't have to look over his shoulder to know what he would find. The smell of blood was enough.

THE EXECUTIONER MADE a swift and deadly entrance into the killing field. Grimaldi had done his part, paving the road to hell. So far, so good. Bolan wasn't about to let his friend down. Old-fashioned nerve and guts were the only things that would save the play here.

Of course their enemies were having something to say about that.

With his M-16 stuttering on full-auto, Bolan made quick work of the troops heading out from the guardhouse hoping to catch Grimaldi with a lucky shot. He took the three hardmen down immediately, zipping them across their backs with a burst of 5.56 mm rounds. They pitched forward, never knowing who or what had blindsided them. He gave the area down by the guardhouse a quick search. Clear. If nothing else, his unopposed entrance meant no one had spotted his earlier departure from the sedan and closure on the gate.

Fair play was never an option in combat. To the south, Grimaldi was drawing heavy fire. Running hard, judging distance to each prong of the ambush, Bolan opted for the closest available target. And it just happened to be the one that could cause Grimaldi the most grief.

A short burst from the M-16 and Bolan hit the searchlight on the control tower, sending out a spray of glass and sparks. He fixed sights on the muzzle-flashes leaping around on the control tower's platform, then checked his rear and found only the dead. Dropping to one knee he slipped a finger around the trigger of the M-203. From above someone let fly a warhead from an RPG-7 that came close to taking out Grimaldi, gouging up turf behind the sedan in a thunderclap of smoky fire.

Bolan let them have it with a 40 mm shell. The grenade streaked, straight and true, hitting the edge of the platform. The fireball took out the control tower and threw mangled bodies in all directions for a swan dive to earth.

Four more down, if his hard scan of round two was on the money. He was betting it was. Four each at the gate, the tower and downrange, all giving Grimaldi a taste of hell.

It was far from over. Bolan still had a good eight-, maybe nine-hundred-meter run before he reached the hangar. The way things had shaped up so far the hard charge could prove an eternity. Once he made the hangar Grimaldi would be on his own for long critical minutes.

Pumping his legs as he hard as he could, the Executioner locked his sights on two gunmen spraying Grimaldi's rear. Autofire rattling the air and the shriek of a jumbo jet lifting off from nearby Sheremetyevo in his ears, Bolan closed hard on the enemy. His heart jackhammered in his chest from the exertion, but as always this was the time, flush in the heat of combat, when he needed to dig even deeper, push it to the limit.

Given the explosion that had reduced the control tower to a smoking skeleton, the two gunmen had it figured someone was coming up their rear. They got it together and were spinning around when Bolan slowed his sprint to a jog and ripped free with the M-16. They were dark shadows when Bolan burned up the clip, mowing them down and sending them on a hard fall beneath flying blood and shredded cloth.

Gathering speed again, Bolan was surging into the fresh killzone when he heard a groan of pain. Searching the area, he found one of the two gunmen Grimaldi had bulldozed, crawling through the grass. The gunman pinned the tall shadow that was Bolan with hate-filled eyes. The hardman's leg was bent at an impossible angle, and the soldier spotted the gleaming shard of shinbone jutting through a tear in his pants. A snarl of either agony or rage as the hardman went for an AK-47, a glutton for punishment. A quick mercy burst and the Executioner ran on.

He had cut another hundred meters to the hangar, then broke into a zigzag. A heartbeat later one, then two divots were blown up by his feet. The lone shooter was on one knee, vaguely outlined atop the hangar by the distant lights of Sheremetyevo.

Bolan picked up the pace, cutting back and forth, giving it all he had.

Ahead, he saw Grimaldi run the sedan on an angle

for the third hangar, covered from the shooter for the moment.

Bolan saw the muzzle-flashes stabbing the gloom in the distance, aimed at Grimaldi's point of cover. The Executioner took a chance that there was only one shooter left. He slapped a fresh clip into his assault rifle, filled the breech of the M-203 with a 40 mm shell and broke into an all-out sprint. Using the grenade launcher would be a last-gasp option. An explosion could mangle the doors, upset the intricate electronic circuitry hooked into the computerized keypad. Of course, they could blow it down, but time was critical. They needed to fly.

The rooftop shooter trained his attention solely on Grimaldi, who was out of the sedan and firing upward with his M-16. The Stony Man pilot hugged the face of the hangar, forging on.

"Come on," Bolan growled to himself, driving his legs as hard as he could, covering the length of one football field after another. Every minute felt an hour, every step earned by raw determination.

Grimaldi and the lone shooter were going at it full blast, burning up one clip after another. The shooter was trying to keep Grimaldi from reaching the electronic keypad, but the pilot went through another clip, driving the shadow enemy to cover. Grimaldi swiped the card through and Bolan saw the hangar doors begin to part. Emergency lights electronically blinked on inside the hangar and Grimaldi took clear shape in Bolan's sight. The soldier figured he had the gap cut to two hundred meters.

Well within range to use either autofire or the M-203.

Bolan went for the grand slam. He dropped to a

knee, saw the shadow draw target acquisition his way. The Executioner aimed for the lip of the roof and let the 40 mm grenade chug away. The shooter was holding back on the trigger of his weapon, then his muzzleflash was lost inside the boiling fireball.

Bolan ran on, called out, "Jack! Jack!"

Grimaldi stepped through the hangar doors. Bolan's friend and fighting comrade looked grim, blood streaking his face.

"Smolenskov?"

"He didn't make it. He bought it from his own side."

That was enough for Bolan. It occurred to him that Smolenskov could have provided a shield for Grimaldi during the hard run. That hadn't been Bolan's intent when leaving the Russian with Grimaldi. Funny how things happened. Smolenskov had been one of the architects behind a nightmare conspiracy that had global implications. Who knew how many he had killed, innocent or otherwise? Certainly there was his war record in Afghanistan, spraying the Afghan natives with nerve gas. Pile up all the narcotics and weapons he had moved, grown rich from and how much misery and ruin had the man heaped on others. No matter. It was a done deal, at least in Russia.

"I'll check the jet for any sign of tampering," Grimaldi said. "Give me three, four minutes tops to get rolling."

The Executioner knew the pilot already had the jet topped up with fuel when they had landed. "Make it quick. I'll make sure it's clear on this end. Let's roll."

"THIS IS WHAT I need, Hal, to wrap this up."

They were airborne, a good sixty minutes south of

Moscow. So far their luck was holding.

Bolan sat portside, just behind the open door to the cockpit, the sat-link on, its console illuminated by a single overhead light.

According to Grimaldi the turbo-fan engines were burning fuel at top speed as the jet cruised twenty-five thousand feet in the air, above the clouds. All lights inside and out, other than the glow from Grimaldi's instrument panel, had been killed. The jet was a ghost ship, flying blind. It was a tactic drug runners often used to avoid detection by the naked eye. Of course, Grimaldi had all the state-of-the-art ECMs, radar and radar-jamming equipment at his command. But this was no fighter jet. With no armament all they could do was hope some hostile MiGs didn't show up and decide to shoot them down. Bolan didn't think that would happen. Stony Man Farm had been hard at work, laying out the next phase, the safest flight path through Russian airspace. Which meant skirting past any military installations and airfields. If there was any damage control to be done in Moscow, Bolan knew Brognola would clean it up.

But Bolan had his enemies running, reeling from the relentless pounding the Stony Man soldiers had inflicted on the Drakovich Family.

On his end Bolan had Brognola up to speed. And from what he had been informed of so far by the big Fed the Stony Man cyberteam had paved their way into Pakistan, and beyond to Yemen.

The soldier gave Brognola his list. "We're going to need an AC-130 gunship. Find a U.S. military base, somewhere along the Saudi-Yemen border. I'm going to need the same HAZMAT team of blacksuits from

New York. Altogether I need a twenty-man team of blacksuits from the Farm, ones with the most combat experience. Rustle up a three-man flight crew to assist Grimaldi with the Spectre. Again blacksuits.''

''I'm already on it. Kurtzman's reading you, loud and clear on this end. You're going to have to give me at least an eighteen-hour window to get this package wrapped up and delivered.''

''The window's closing on this one,'' Bolan said. ''This missing SS-20 entered the picture. My guess is the Drakovich heirs have the PALs to that missile and they're flying there now to sell the codes to this renegade Colonel Tuhbat.''

''About that, we anticipated some of your moves on this end. I've already called in a lot of favors—I'll spare you the alphabet soup list. Anyway, the GRU and the CIA have apparently known about this SS-20 for some time. They have a team in place, as we speak, in Karachi. I've got a contact for you, an ISI agent, one Major Mohammed Buhjwabi of the Pakistani military intelligence service. He'll be ready and waiting for you when you hit Karachi. Run with his program. The Russians are understandably embarrassed about this SS-20 fiasco. Usually they send in a team of Spetsnaz commandos to clean up the garbage their own leave in the yard. This time is no different. I got you and Grimaldi inserted on the ISI team, but you're only in charge of yourselves. My CIA contact in Pakistan says the Pakistanis would like to keep this SS-20 situation from leaking out to the rest of the world, says they've had enough bad press and publicity problems lately.''

''Good enough, but Karachi's one party we can't afford to miss. If I can nail the Drakovich heirs, the

Russian Mafia thorn can be pulled. On to Yemen. How about those satellite pics of the site in question?"

"They're coming through now. I'll get the whole package put together and fax it to you. Give me a few more minutes. It's incredible," Brognola suddenly said, and Bolan heard the weariness and anxiety in the big Fed's voice. "I mean how this could have been kept under the carpet all these years. Payoffs most likely, or a bullet with the name on it of someone unwilling to go with the program. Anyway, we've pored over the site in question. To the untrained eye I can see how it might pass for an oil site. You've got derricks, pipelines, drilling and digging machinery…anyway, some digging around and we found this Russian company, Vladovich, moved in the heavy machinery at the time in question. So the part about them being able to smuggle in the component parts to build a reprocessing plant is well within the realm of possibility. Scratch that, it's happened. Hell, forget political backlash—if the Israelis got wind of this, they'd B-52 Yemen back into the Stone Age, maybe even a surgical nuclear strike that would chernobylize the country for a thousand years."

"That's only one reason I want this kept to the home team."

"One quick aside. The warehouse that blew up and nearly took out the FBI team, well, their forensics guys say there must have been enough plastic explosive already housed there, on top of what you believed the one hostile brought to the party, to take out a whole block. Who knows? Maybe the Drakovich Family was also moving plastic explosives. But the FBI forensics boys found large residue traces of ether, kerosene and acetone. Looks like our late Don was definitely moving precursor chemicals used to make cocaine. The late Don was a very busy man.''

"Now that you mention it, I do recall smelling a chemical taint in the air. It only makes more sense now why they were willing to risk it all, even if it meant cutting some losses, in terms of money and mules. Anyway…''

"Ancient history. Okay, Striker, here comes the intel package you need. We need this one wrapped quickly. I won't sleep again until that reprocessing plant is knocked out and you two are on your way home. Good luck.''

The Executioner was all too aware they would need more than just a smile from the gods once they hit Yemen. He waited as the fax machine began to spill out what he would need to pave the road to hell for his enemies.

15

Bolan and Grimaldi were no strangers to Pakistan. The Muslim country was a familiar bloody turf—a nation that had seen countless riots and more than a couple of revolutions, put down only when brutal martial law swept the country, a country that wielded the fourth largest army in the world, slugging out several wars with its hated and feared neighbor, India, over the disputed Kashmir. Ferocious engagements of mass and eventual indiscriminate slaughter that carried over to the civilian population helped propel the Pakistanis into the nuclear arms race. Pakistan: Where a male stranger could be shot on sight if he spoke to a veiled woman. Where public flogging and mutilation were the order of the day for convicted criminals. Where segments of the military and the police were well-known for always having a hand out. All that, and then some from a country that was barely over fifty years old.

A grim picture, but Bolan was feeling that way, had been since touching down outside Karachi and disembarking from the jet to be greeted by their waiting ISI contact. That had been almost twelve hours ago, and the Executioner's adrenaline was still running hot. At this point, time didn't aid and abet their campaign. Already the sun was setting over Karachi Harbor.

And still no sign of their targets.

Bolan scoured the face of ISI Major Mohammed Buhjwabi. It was hard to get a clear fix on the man, but the Executioner sensed he was dealing with a balls to the wall, no-nonsense soldier, backboned by principle, out to do only the right thing, both for personal honor and love of country. The tall, lean major, dressed in black with an Heckler & Koch MP-5 submachine gun slung from his shoulder, was surveying the waterfront and surrounding warehouses through binoculars. Between searches, he checked his watch, all scowls and tension. Bolan could well appreciate the major's desire to get on with it, the anxiety that always came before facing heavily armed competition.

They were on the second story of a warehouse, maybe a block west of another warehouse where Buhjwabi's eyes and ears said the meeting between the renegade Colonel Tuhbat and the Drakovich sons would go down.

Naturally the waiting and chewing on precombat nerves was the worst part. The ISI major knew Bolan had been hard at work terrorizing the Drakovich organization, but both sides had only filled the other in on a need-to-know basis. Buhjwabi wanted the SS-20 out of his country, and Bolan wanted the heads of Vlad and Gregor Drakovich. They came to a mutual understanding of sorts, with the major making no guarantees that special agents Belasko or Grisham would be the ones to nail the Russian Dons when the bullets starting flying. Fair enough. But Bolan needed this wrapped up, aware Brognola and the Stony Man team had shored up the details for a final showdown in Yemen.

First this Pakistan foray. Bolan had already been informed by Buhjwabi that the joint CIA-Spetsnaz force was ready to descend on a remote village north of

Karachi where the SS-20 was known to be housed. Whenever the renegade Tuhbat arrived, Buhjwabi would radio the strike force to proceed as planned and seize the SS-20 by any and all available means.

Their own plan of attack was in line with keep-it-simple. The sniper team consisted of two ISI agents on another warehouse rooftop, covering the east end of the target building. Two more two-man observation-sniper teams, south and north, were ready to drop any sentries outside while the meet took place and the strike force moved in. A nice triangulated field of fire that could also catch any runners fleeing the scene. Six more ISI agents, donning work clothes of dockworkers, were out on the wharf, covering the west end if the action spilled out that way.

The enemy numbers were sketchy. The major's ballpark figure was thirty, no more than forty between both Russians and renegade Pakistanis. The problem was there had been no sighting of the Russians or their aircraft, so a solid fix on numbers was guesswork. Bolan was betting the Russian opposition had made their way into Pakistan—a tried-and-true smuggler's flight path, then a secured route by vehicle into the city—using military and police contacts corrupted by blood money. Whether it was wishful thinking, instinct or both, the Executioner could almost feel the Russian gangsters out there in the city, heading their way.

Bolan gave the ISI team a quick once-over. They were dressed in black, Heckler & Koch MP-5s, sidearms, comm-links with throat mikes. Sixteen altogether, including their American visitors.

At this point, Bolan didn't care which side got hold of the nuclear missile. Naturally Spetsnaz owned the rights to take the SS-20 back to Russia. But from what he'd seen of his FSK comrades in Russia Bolan couldn't be one hundred percent sure the missile would make it into uncompromised possession. Whatever, the matter had been taken out of his hands. What he suspected was one or both of the Drakovich sons had the PALs to the SS-20, and the codes were up for sale. For that reason alone, the Executioner needed to see Vlad and Gregor Drakovich terminated. This was a take-no-prisoners outing. Once he severed the final heads of the hydra of this particular Russian Mafia Family he could move on to Yemen, disrupt the bidding war and knock out the reprocessing plant.

Easier said than proved, of course.

"Something you would like to say, Agent Belasko?"

Bolan had a lot to say to Major Buhjwabi as he met the man's dark stare. But he kept it simple, believing he had all the facts about the operation as the ISI knew them.

"The lack of choppers. In a city this size, not knowing how many guns we're dealing with, or their contingency plans if they bolt or manage a fighting withdrawal, well, a little aerial support would lend a helping hand to those of us down here."

"That was my call. No helicopters. I don't want to spook our targets if they see gunships hovering all around the harbor. This Colonel Tuhbat is slippery but he can also strike like a cobra when you least expect it. The man is a menace," the major said, and Bolan read loud and clear the hatred in the man's voice for the renegade colonel.

When he first heard the name, Tuhbat, it rang a bell in Bolan's head. The Executioner had once before gone up against a similarly named and now deceased foe in

Pakistan. Turned out this Tuhbat was a distant cousin of the dead man in question. Same army rank, almost the same name. Small world, Bolan reasoned. It seemed the lust for riches reaped from the blood and misery of others ran in the family.

Buhjwabi squared his shoulders, as if daring Bolan to dispute his claim to the man. "He is a blight on my country. He has disgraced himself and all Pakistanis, and I must tell you, he's the reason the Russian criminals have been able to so easily corrupt my fellow countrymen. I heard you ask about these Russian criminals and why the ISI or the army hasn't been able to find them once they flew into Pakistani airspace. I believe the matter is easily, if not painfully put to rest. They have bought silence and blindness. Now, if at all possible, I want this Pakistani criminal taken alive. I want to see him tried, convicted and hanged. What happens to the mercenaries he'll bring, I don't care—it will be open season on them. The more of them dead, the better."

Bolan gave the major's anger and determination a simple nod.

The handheld radio crackled to life on Buhjwabi's belt. A voice came through, speaking in Urdu, calling on the major in the official tongue of Pakistan. Bolan listened, not knowing the language all that well, but read the shadow of grim determination falling over the major's face.

The strike force around Bolan came alive.

The Executioner glimpsed Grimaldi giving him a knowing look, the Stony Man pilot ready to go. Bolan was searching the winding maze of alleys and archways that stretched out from their surveillance point.

To the north he spotted a minicaravan of Jeeps and trucks rolling their way.

Buhjwabi signed off and Bolan looked the major dead in the eye.

"A moment while I inform the CIA-Spetsnaz team they can move in. Wait then until all targets are inside the warehouse. When I give the order, then it will be as you Americans would say, 'show time.'"

The Executioner and Grimaldi hauled up their M-16/ M-203 combos.

Pakistan was about to get another taste of riot and revolution, only this time it would be Executioner style.

"THAT TUNNEL had better be where you say it is. Are we clear, Mujwhal?"

Vlad Drakovich heard the steely edge in his brother's voice, but had to look at Gregor twice to be sure he was reading correctly the veiled threat, the undercurrent of menace that snapped him to attention. He could understand his younger brother's shaky nerves, but Gregor wore a new look of raw determination.

The new Don wanted a show of guts, all right, the nerve to kill on demand to be enough to get them through. He had already laid it out for his people. But Gregor was no cold-blooded killer, and if what Muhjwal and their father's man in Pakistan, Viktor Dtechka, had informed them was true, the meet with Tuhbat was a done deal before it even got started. The bastard had betrayed the Family. The missile had been moved from the colonel's warehouse, something that went expressly against his father's wishes, Dtechka had told him. Tuhbat was holding out, playing games, and he was about to pay the ultimate price.

For Vlad Drakovich it was more than enough that

he was simply ready to unleash all the fear, rage and pain he had suffered the past few days. Another search of Gregor's new look, and Vlad thought there might be hope for his brother yet. If nothing else he sensed Gregor was ready to do some much-needed killing himself. A definite plus, knowing they were motivated to see this through, his way, on the same page. Under different circumstances Vlad would have clasped his brother on the shoulders, planted a kiss on each cheek for his new and approved stance.

Then the crime boss gave the drainage pipe in question a hard search. It was a hole that jutted out the side of an embankment on what passed for a sandy stretch of beach. Just large enough, he observed, for a man to squeeze through at normal height. As the wind blew his way, he caught a whiff of sewage and chemicals spilling from the hole. This was a sprawling warehouse-industrial district and he could be sure all manner of poisons were oozing out that hole. Trying to picture the hit in his mind, seeing it all in the mind's eye before executing, he indulged a moment of silence. Out on the harbor the big ships chugged along at a snail's pace. The skyline of Karachi, a bizarre mix of gleaming skyscrapers, mosques and grim-looking apartment buildings, loomed in the twilight sky to the north. He had never before been to Pakistan. Any business dealings using Tuhbat and moving heroin into Russia had always been handled through intermediaries.

Vlad Drakovich softly shook his head, weary all of a sudden, wondering if his anger and drive were fading with lost time and jumpy nerves. It had been a long flight before landing at the remote and secured airstrip west of the city. So far the contacts and groundwork laid out in his father's will were holding up.

Time to go to work. At the top of a sandy hill, Vlad looked at the two-man team he would leave behind with their vans and Jeeps. He hoped what he had on hand and inside himself would be enough to see them through the killing he knew was just ahead, then get them clear of the country without a small army of enraged Pakistanis on their heels, howling for blood. He would take a handheld radio, his Uzi submachine, eighteen soldiers to the warehouse. He was there to honor his father's will, and his name, or die in the attempt.

An hour ago he had contacted Tuhbat, who was en route for the meet. The boss recalled the strain he'd heard in Tuhbat's voice, but managed to keep his own tone neutral. Business as usual.

Vlad Drakovich searched the swarthy bearded face of Mujwhal, waiting for the Pakistani to answer his brother.

"I believe my brother asked you a question."

Mujwhal scowled, pulled back his long hair to reveal a missing ear. Nothing more than a black hole ringed by dead purple flesh showed where his ear used to be.

"Do you see this?" Mujwhal snarled. "I was once a friend and confidant of Tuhbat's. I attempted to strike a drug deal on my own, maybe a year ago. I had a family to feed, and I felt I deserved more than dog scraps. It was my deal, my shipment, paid for out of my pocket. However, Tuhbat didn't care for my sense of independence, my desire to see my wife and ten children have something of a future. He had his men hold me down, and he sliced off my ear. A week later, he had my entire family murdered. Do you know what he said? 'Living,' he said, 'would be far more painful a punishment for me than simply being executed.' The fool! He let me live, dismissed me as if I was nothing more than some boot-licking lackey. Everything I have done for you isn't for you. I wish to see this man dead.''

That was good enough for Vlad Drakovich. These days he understood that kind of hate.

''How far from here?''

''It's a mile hike north,'' Mujwhal said.

Gregor Drakovich was having trouble buying the whole setup. He looked at the short bulldog figure of Viktor Dtechka. ''Comrade?''

''I have been a loyal soldier for your father here in Pakistan for years. I know Mujwhal. You can trust him.''

''We do, Comrade,'' Vlad Drakovich said, ''with our lives.''

Just the same, Vlad Drakovich ordered three of his heavily armed troops to move in on the warehouse from the drainage pipe. It couldn't hurt to cover all angles, then throw a back-door surprise at the Pakistanis. Not only that, but he would know if Mujwhal was being straight with him about the trapdoor that led from the north end of the warehouse to the drainage pipe. As they headed off, Vlad Drakovich told the three-man hit team to make every flying bullet count when the shooting started.

He took a moment to regard his brother. The brothers Drakovich looked at each other, long and hard, sharing a private moment of renewed trust, feeling some unbreakable bond between them. Vlad gave his sibling a smile, a genuine expression he felt straight from the heart, something he hadn't thought he'd ever feel for a brother he'd felt couldn't quite cut it in their world.

Vlad Drakovich felt inspired.

16

Fueled by murder in his heart and pumped on knowledge his mind was right, the Russian Boss led his brother and their small army into the warehouse. Vlad Drakovich ignored the suspicious looks the twenty or so Pakistanis were laying on them. They openly displayed the hardware of their business partners from Moscow.

Vlad fought down the strange urge to laugh out loud, smear his contempt for them in their faces. He didn't give a damn how many of them they had to face down or how heavily armed the opposition was. He didn't give a damn about the SS-20 either. Tuhbat could keep it, suck on that missile and go straight to hell. The Family would just have to cut their losses and move on, learning from another bitter lesson. There were a lot of hard truths being shoved down his throat these days, but this would be the last one he suffered, he told himself. Without the access codes, which he would jealously guard to a last bitter breath if necessary, the SS-20 was a useless scrap of steel anyway. Without him, he thought, no one could win and taste the fat payday. No Vlad, no missile.

Vlad Drakovich controlled, even owned the destinies of men, indeed, perhaps even whole nations, maybe even the world.

His orders were clear, his men knew what to do and would follow him to the gates of hell if called upon to do so. Mujwhal was ordered to hang back for a full minute while the Boss set the stage. There was no point tipping his hand right off. That he had radioed his men in the tunnel, knew they were in place already was a plus. The tunnel was his genie in the bottle to uncap on the rear guard. Not only that, it was their way out, since the Boss didn't care to evacuate in open ground after settling up this unpleasant but necessary piece of business. Someone in the vicinity, dockworker, passerby, whatever, was bound to alert the authorities once the shooting started. Worse, the treacherous Tuhbat might even have snipers posted on the rooftop of another warehouse, some rear guard waiting in case it hit the fan. Outside it had all looked normal enough, but Vlad Drakovich had seen too many setbacks, choked down too much bile of bitter defeats in the past few days to take anything at face value.

This would be his way to launch the organization back on track. It would be a major coup, killing Tuhbat. A crowning achievement, of sorts, but certainly a way to warn all their business associates from as far away as the Golden Triangle that Vlad Drakovich was in charge, and not a man to be fucked with.

"Comrade Dtechka, greetings. I see you have worked things out again. A Russian operating on Pakistani soil, no small feat."

If the guy only knew, the Boss thought. Uzi slung from his shoulder, cocked and locked, Vlad Drakovich took up point. He stopped ten yards or so from the tall man in the black leather bomber jacket. He had seen a picture of the infamous Colonel Atta Tuhbat. The man was medium height, broad shoulders, close-cut black hair, beard and mustache, hawkish face and the burning eyes of a fanatic. The man looked, even reeked of treachery to the Boss. Hats off to Dtechka, their man in Pakistan, with a little help from Mujwhal.

There was hard silence, tension heating up the air all around, as Tuhbat watched with angry eyes while the Russians fanned out. From the corner of his eye, Vlad spotted his younger brother slowly making his way around the far flanks of the tightly packed group around the Pakistani colonel.

"You must be Vlad Drakovich," the Colonel said, an edge in his voice. He looked then at Gregor. "And you, Gregor. I understand you have had some trouble."

"Good news travels to your doorstep very fast," Vlad said.

The colonel didn't how to take that, squared his shoulders and jutted his chin. "I'm sorry about what happened to your father. I did much business with him for many years. Ours was a very profitable relationship. He will be missed."

The Boss got right to it, after a quick search of the warehouse. Pallets, crates, steel containers, forklifts and other machinery were spread around. Nobody was up on the catwalks, although he'd seen the two Pakistanis outside, watching the store with AK-47s ready. The numbers were fairly even, give or take a couple of guns. No matter, this was a done deal.

"Spare me the kissing of ass. I understand you moved the missile."

Tuhbat cleared his throat, and the Boss saw the man's hand sliding down to his AK-47.

"I understand you disobeyed my father's express wish, which was to leave the missile here in this warehouse."

"Would you ask your men to stop moving? You're beginning to make me very uncomfortable."

"Fuck your discomfort. I understand you don't want to come up with the agreed-upon price for the missile."

Tuhbat's gaze narrowed, the look of a cornered animal. "I can't possibly come up with that much money. Perhaps if you handed over the access codes we could reason out some compromise."

"I don't compromise, Colonel."

Gregor moved up on the rear of the Pakistanis, reaching inside his coat for the mini-Uzi. The new Gregor was ready to kill. Vlad liked what he saw. The past was a bitter pill of rivalry and jealousy born of pure greed and desire, but from this moment on, he determined Gregor would be his equal.

"Yes, I have the codes." Vlad Drakovich tapped the side of his head. "And they are for sale. But only if the price is right."

"This isn't good. As a good-faith measure I'm willing to give you five million dollars in American cash—once I have the codes."

"Not good enough."

Tuhbat bared his teeth. "Listen to me, you little—I sent six men on to Yemen."

That was news to him, but the Boss could check that out easily enough. He didn't need any more surprises.

"They have another two million in American dollars ready to be delivered as another good-faith measure. I want first shot at what you have produced at the facility. Your father would want as much. We had an arrangement."

Vlad Drakovich chuckled. "Two million? Is that all? I don't think my father would have settled for such an insulting offer. My father is dead, as you well know, and now you must meet my terms." He chuckled again. "You must think I have no head for business. You must think I'm some spoiled child that can be pushed around by you, patted on the head and appeased by your offer that is nothing more than a candy bar."

"I can't say I care for your attitude. You're in my country, the missile is here and you will deal with me."

"Do I hear an 'or else' there, Colonel?"

"Yes! Damn you!"

The look, the grim smile on Tuhbat's lips told the Boss that Mujwhal had just made his grand entrance.

A second later, he was sure of it as the Boss heard from behind, "Hello, Colonel."

Tuhbat nodded, knowing the deal, and it was a bad one. "I understand how things are now, Comrades."

The colonel moved to pull the assault rifle off his shoulder.

"Then you can take your offer to hell with you," Vlad Drakovich said, giving the catchphrase, hauling the Uzi off his shoulder in one lightning-smooth motion.

The Pakistanis were a little slow in getting it together, perhaps stunned that their Russian partners were making some grandstand play, all balls and indifference to consequence. It proved their tough luck. A fatal error in judgment.

The Boss cut loose with his Uzi SMG, in sync with his younger brother, who began unleashing a wave of 9 mm Parabellum rounds to their rear. All about him the sound of weapon fire shattered Vlad Drakovich's senses. Tuhbat was the first to go. The colonel toppled, his AK-47 barking and flaming away as at least a dozen bullets were walked across his chest. Tuhbat went down hard with a howl of rage, his flailing body rained on by his own juices.

The Boss felt good, in the thick of it, taking the blood he wanted. He was light-headed, nearly giddy, as all the fear, hatred and pain he had endured since Brighton Beach was being vented, pouring out of him from his blazing Uzi.

The Pakistanis were like some bad chorus line in his death sights, jerking and twitching, absorbing lead. The Russians and Mujwhal poured it on, and for just a heartbeat the Boss found it too easy. Then return fire from Pakistanis braving their last stand reached out and took blood. The Pakistanis were catching lead and spouting gore, but managed to nail several of the Russians. Drakovich caught a glimpse of bloody figures pitching beside him.

Vlad Drakovich sidled away from the tracking autofire, but heard the bullets whisper past his ears. He held back on the Uzi's trigger, burned through the magazine, reloaded quickly. A few of the wiser and luckier Pakistanis made a desperate flight for cover. Several of them made it. Sharp cries of pain hit the Boss's ears, he knew the enemy had scored a few more kills. It was no time to assess casualties.

That line of thinking changed in the next moment. And it all soured as Vlad Drakovich saw his world further ripped apart.

Sweeping the Uzi back and forth, scoring flesh and savoring his moment of victory nearly at hand, Vlad Drakovich thought he heard his brother cry out but couldn't be sure with all the racket of weapons, the chaos and confusion of combat. Suddenly, from beyond the falling tangle of limbs and dying men, he saw Gregor dropping, blood flying from his chest. *Oh, no, oh, no,* Vlad Drakovich heard his mind scream, his limbs locked up for an eternal second. It couldn't be, it wasn't.

"Move out! Move out!" the Boss shouted at his survivors. As he ran for the twitching form of his brother, he waxed another Pakistani on the fly with a quick triburst from his submachine gun. The world spun in his eyes, even as time seemed to freeze. Rage and grief burned through every fiber of his being as the horror of the moment seized him. He knelt beside Gregor, as bullets singed the air dangerously close behind him. He couldn't be sure, in the heat of combat, but a sickening thought danced through his mind, wanting to paralyze him. He tried to shake the ugly thought away, throwing his head from side to side, but couldn't. It hung there, a laughing voice, taunting him.

Was it his bullet that had struck down his brother?

"Gregor? Gregor!"

The whites of Gregor's eyes showed as he desperately sucked for air. A hand shot out, and it took another long moment before he realized his younger brother was grabbing him, fingers like steel talons digging into his flesh.

"Did you...get...what you came here...for...?"

Vlad Drakovich screamed, "Don't die! Don't you die on me!"

THE EXECUTIONER and Grimaldi were the first ones through the door, leading a four-man ISI team assigned to them. For the Americans this was meant to be their curtain call on the Drakovich heirs as they made their play from the east door.

Bolan found the party was already well under way, and he feared he was too late for the show.

Moments ago, as a sniper team dropped the two sentries with head shots from sound-suppressed rifles, the shooting erupted inside the warehouse. The major gave the order over his earpiece, and Bolan and Grimaldi, donning gas masks, went through the door and found a vision of hell on earth greeting them. Flash-stun grenades had already paved the way in, and Bolan and Grimaldi rode out the thunder, having closed their eyes as the blinding white supernovas hit the combatants in the middle of the warehouse. Tear-gas canisters were then pitched by Bolan, Grimaldi and friendlies while more gas clouds burst through the air from Major Buhjwabi's point of attack from the west, adding to the pandemonium.

The soldier quickly found this wasn't amateur night. They were gagging and choking, reeling all over the place, but still firing away for all they were worth, holding their ground, bulldogging through their pain and shock to fling it back in the faces of their attackers.

Bolan, Grimaldi and his team peeled off. The Americans were moving in one direction while the ISI agents raced off for a pile of crates, seeking cover, picking targets.

There wasn't much left to shoot down, but the few survivors were giving it their all.

Bullets drilled the stone wall above Bolan's head as shadowy figures staggered through the dense haze. It was difficult to tell who was who, but Bolan got busy firing at the opposition, his M-16 sweeping left to right, aiming for the AK-47s favored by the competition. With Grimaldi firing away with his own M-16 from his right flank, the two soldiers dropped a trio of hardmen, the fiery muzzle-flashes piercing smoke before the guns fell silent and dead bodies hit the floor, twitched out.

From concealment behind a forklift and a pile of crates several hardmen were holding back the storm, sweeping lead in all directions, wild but potentially fatal bursts just the same.

It chewed up close to three minutes or more, as Bolan, Grimaldi and the ISI strike force closed in on the survivors, burning through two magazines, seeking out points of attack. It was hard for Bolan to tell if they were Pakistani or Russian, but whoever was holding their ground was willing to go down fighting.

They were blinded, their senses shattered and eyes tearing, of course, but they were like automatons, full of some suicidal frenzy, driven by fear and shock.

It took some doing, but the combined Stony Man–ISI strike force finally silenced the enemy guns.

Too much critical time was lost and Bolan sensed something wasn't right.

With his ears ringing, Bolan searched the killzone for wounded, any possum looking to rise. There were no takers.

It was a clean sweep.

A search of the bodies, as the gas clouds thinned, and Bolan couldn't find either Drakovich. And he had clearly seen them march into the warehouse before the major gave the word to move out from their surveillance position.

Bolan heard Buhjwabi barking orders to his men. Giving Grimaldi the word to begin his own hunt, Bolan began moving up and down the aisles between the crates, containers and pallets, M-16 fanning and ready to fire. Several dead Pakistanis and Russians were strewed along the way.

No Drakovich heirs.

A good five agonizing minutes passed before Bolan

walked back to the major, who stood seething over a bullet-riddled corpse. He kicked the body, his snarl muffled by his gas mask. Bolan met the major's angry stare as Buhjwabi told him, "The bastard got off too easy."

Forget Tuhbat, the soldier thought. *The guy is history.*

"The Drakoviches?" Bolan posed.

"I don't know," Buhjwabi growled. "We're searching now."

"Anyone make it out on the docks?"

"No."

Silently Bolan cursed. He found Grimaldi walking up to him, coming from an aisle to the north.

"I've got something, Striker."

Bolan didn't like the sound of that.

THE FEELING of anguish this time was worse, burned deeper than the fires of hate and grief that he had experienced over the news of their father's death. Vlad Drakovich didn't understand this new and profound sorrow, how he had suddenly come to value the life of his brother more than his father's.

Not that it mattered in the long run.

His younger brother was dead.

This new horrifying twist didn't end his thoughts of fury, hate and vengeance. Some fiery nagging ripped apart his soul, eating him up as if acid had been forced down his throat. No, he couldn't help but wonder if his finger had pulled the trigger, sending the bullet that had ended Gregor's life. It was possible he had accidentally, in the heat of battle, killed his brother. Of course, he'd never know for sure, so he vowed from that moment on not to think about it. His continued survival was all that mattered. If he died, his father's dream would die, at best the project taken over by less capable hands, men of greed and ruthlessness who didn't care about the Family, but wanted only power and dominion. But wasn't that what he was after? No. No chance, no way. He was different. He was simply honoring his father's request, the eldest son with a clearly defined objective. Now the last of the bloodline.

He wanted to wail over this new horror, but he didn't dare. His surviving force and Dtechka were counting on him to get them clear of the harbor, and out of Karachi. Even so, this was more reason to fulfill his father's wishes, no matter what it took, damn the risk.

It was little comfort, given the burden he carried, but at least his Pakistani enemies lay slain by his hand. Still, the future, he knew, held more enemies to confront, more blood to shed. No risk, no gain.

He couldn't fail, he must not fail. Face had been saved, but at a heavy price.

Vlad Drakovich squeezed down the tunnel, his brother's corpse scraping the walls, holding him down to a snail's pace. His heart felt like a raging ball of fire in his chest. His nose was knifed by a mixed bag of stench and he tried to breathe through his mouth, the air, coming in and out, a ragged gasp. Chemicals and sewage, the bitter smell of fear assaulted his senses as they slogged through the slime, with a lone flashlight and Dtechka leading the retreat.

Last and certainly not least was the coppery sting of Gregor's blood in his nose.

The smell of defeat.

The scene kept wanting to replay itself through his mind even as he tried to will away the image of his brother falling, and perhaps by his own hand. It was too much to bear. For the first time in his life, Vlad Drakovich thought he might break, hit his knees, weep like some mother over a dead son. *Keep going, stay strong,* he commanded himself. He was still alive, a leader of men, a warrior. And the dead were counting on him. He could hear them urging him on, from the beyond, in the blackness and stench of the tunnel. Their blood wouldn't be shed in vain.

Each step, hauling the limp weight of Gregor, was earned with great and raging determination. Under the threat of death, he had given the order for two of his men to lag behind. If the attackers, whoever they were, opened the trapdoor, they were to fire away and cover their withdrawal. They were sacrificing themselves, of course, but they knew the deal going in, the risks involved if they didn't obey his orders. If the ones left behind lived and made it out of Pakistan somehow, they knew their future was paved with gold.

Something like a series of thunderclaps, something that had burned the air and lanced the eyes like an exploding sun had hit his senses, nearly knocking him to the floor.

A hit, planned and executed on the meet. Visions of their American problem danced through his mind. How could it be? Or were the Pakistani authorities making a raid?

"You must leave him, put him down. Please, Vlad, we need to get out of this tunnel and out of this country!"

It took a few moments before Dtechka's plea cut through the ringing in his ears, the searing memory of the last awful minutes in the warehouse.

Under other circumstances, he would have shot the man dead for this impertinence. But he realized time was critical. Dtechka was right about the need for haste. In the eerie glow of the flashlight ahead, Vlad Drakovich met the man's grim stare and nodded.

Gently, he laid his brother in the muck. It was an insult, another ugly piece of reality, putting his brother's dead body in raw sewage and chemicals that would quickly eat the flesh from his bones. What could he do? Survival was the only thing that mattered.

He closed his brother's eyelids, kissed him on the cheek, ignoring the tension and impatience around him. "Goodbye, my brother. I will avenge this. You have my word."

THE TRAIL OF BLOOD led right to the trapdoor. Bolan gave the exit a hard look, feeling the edges, then lifting the door an inch in search of trip wires. No booby trap, at least not one of a human kind. He had seen this kind of safety valve before, and suspected what he would find in short order.

"Step back!" the Executioner ordered Grimaldi and the ISI strike force. They cleared the area and Bolan flung the trapdoor wide. Muzzle-flashes from snarling weapons pierced the dark down there, and bullets sailed harmlessly toward the ceiling.

The Executioner took a frag grenade, armed it, then counted off the doomsday numbers and dropped it in the hole.

Smoke, fire and pieces of flesh and shredded cloth exploded up from the hole. With his gas mask off, Bolan smelled the blood and cordite from the smoking dark below. For good measure he dropped another grenade, rode out the blast, then hopped down the hole, M-16 poised.

Two shredded bodies stretched out beneath Bolan.

Peering beyond the smoke, he searched the darkness, the stillness far down the tunnel. It was quiet, so silent down there he felt a sense of frustration and anger dropping over him. Looking up, he saw Grimaldi and the ISI major staring down at him.

The Executioner's grim silence and angry look said it all.

The prime targets were long gone.

17

It struck him as something of an SOS call, an eleventh-hour alert to scramble the troops, secure their money, then begin the bargaining for the finished product, or else. The son of the late Yuri Drakovich didn't come right out and say he was running—or rather flying—to Yemen in fear of his life, but Igor Pavlovka noted the strain in Vlad Drakovich's voice. There was a strange undertone of panic or anger, something he couldn't quite put his finger on. Something was happening, and Pavlovka knew it wasn't good. There were problems on the other end, but he could tell the new boss wasn't going to hand out any details. Judging what little facts he was getting, it was all need-to-know on the boss's end, but for damn sure, Pavlovka needed to know something.

The Russian listened to his standing orders while hunched over the laptop, earpiece in, fingers grasping the minimike poised at his lips. He glanced over his shoulder at Alexi and Sergei, the two men armed with their tried-and-true AK-47s. They stood beside the window, the curtains closed. As ordered, the windows in every room of their floor were to remain shut, curtains closed at all times. The CIA were crawling all over Aden, like human cockroaches. His sources in the port city had confirmed this, but he had seen them himself across the street earlier in the evening, acting as if they were mere tourists, then occasionally eyeballing the fourth floor. A bulge of a weapon was visible beneath their jackets. And who the hell wore jackets in this kind of heat anyway? Of course, shutting the windows only raised the room temperature another ten stifling degrees, heating Pavlovka's blood even more for action. But added discomfort was a slightly more tolerable option than having the spooks use their listening devices to eavesdrop on his room. Of course, the Russian knew the spooks had sophisticated listening devices that could easily penetrate a thin pane of glass, but the windows would stay shut just the same, out of paranoia more than reason.

A bad feeling suddenly washed over Pavlovka, warning him this was going to be a long and very bad night.

"Yes, yes, I understand," he said. "We'll meet you at the site in five hours. Understood. I have twenty of our people on-site, along with another twenty Yemeni soldiers who have been helping to guard the complex." It was curious, he thought, the new boss asking how many guns were available. Trouble, no doubt, was being dumped in his lap.

Then he heard Drakovich ask about who had come through with what kind of money. Fortunately there was some good news to report on that item. Pavlovka dropped a gaze on the duffel bag by his feet, bulging with cash, one of a dozen bags the prince's cronies had brought in that afternoon. There were duffel bags and suitcases all over the Saudi's room now, more money than he had ever seen in his wildest fantasies, he told Drakovich. Yes, the Somali warlord had four million and promised more in the future. Vlad grunted on the other end. Not enough. Pavlovka understood. This was no time for promises or heated pledges for future payments. It was put up or shut up.

The best news was the Saudi prince had come up with fifteen million, cash, half of which, the ex-KGB reported, had been moved ahead to the complex with three of his most trusted and capable men. That was wise, Vlad had told him. All that money lying around, well, he could never be too careful. And the merchandise, Pavlovka's man on-site had reported, was ready to be sold and shipped out. He heard Vlad Drakovich complain that the money on hand was a woefully small amount, all things considered. Pavlovka had to agree, and told the new boss as much. After all the years of struggle and toil, there now seemed to be very little reward on the table for their combined efforts.

"I intend to change that, and take what is rightfully ours," he heard Vlad Drakovich inform him. "What else do I need to know before we arrive?"

"The Pakistanis arrived this afternoon."

Pavlovka heard the hesitation on the other end, then the anger and fear in the new boss's voice cranked up a notch.

"How many?"

"Six."

"How much money did they bring?"

"We counted two million. American."

"Where are they now?"

"In the room with the prince," Pavlovka said. "I have ordered all bidding parties to gather in the prince's room. All remaining money is being counted as we speak."

"This is what you are to do. You'll follow my orders, Comrade, or pay the penalty of severe punishment if you fail.''

Pavlovka listened, quickly feeling his blood run hot. When he heard what Vlad Drakovich ordered him to do he wasn't sure if he was heated up from fear or excitement.

THE TALL SHADOW moved toward the old and battered hotel, cutting swiftly across the broad avenue, the sound of nightlife swirling around him. Even at that late hour the merchants were still out in force, hawking their wares. The Executioner steeled his mind to the task ahead.

It had been no small feat getting into Yemen. The CIA contacts set up by Brognola had come through, from the desert pickup to weapons and hard intel on a bidding war now under way in this nameless hotel in Aden. For months, the CIA had had the hotel's occupants—the Russians, the Saudi prince and Hezbollah cronies, the Somali warlord and others—under surveillance. But the CIA couldn't act against this bizarre smorgasbord of foreigners in any official or even unofficial capacity without creating a messy international incident.

The Executioner wasn't saddled with that problem.

The soldier had the layout of the hotel, the enemy numbers and some hard facts about whom he could expect to find on the fourth floor of the hotel. The CIA contacts had worked hard, even risked their lives to get Bolan to this stage. He wasn't about to let their efforts go to waste. Beneath his loose-fitting jacket he carried his Beretta 93-R, and an Ingram MAC-10 submachine gun in a special shoulder rig. Both weapons were fixed with sound suppressors. In his coat pocket the soldier had one flash-stun grenade, one frag grenade. Spare clips were tucked in his waistband and a commando dagger sheathed on his hip. He was going for a surprise entrance, hoping stealth, daring and a quick shave of the numbers would tip the scales in his favor.

It was far from being a lock. Getting the job done here, then driving back by Jeep to the site where his strike force would parachute in for a dawn raid on the nuclear reprocessing complex would be cutting it close. Their base of operations had already been established on the Saudi-Yemen border, and Bolan had to tip his hat to Brognola for coming through with men and material in the pinch. During the flight in the AC-130 for his combat jump to the waiting CIA contact in the remote desert north of Aden, Bolan had pored over the satellite pics and all the intel gathered on the hardsite. Then he briefed his blacksuit strike force on the battle strategy. While Bolan did his solo act in Aden to further shatter the dreams of his enemies, Grimaldi and crew would fly back to the border.

The Executioner knew Vlad Drakovich had made it out of Pakistan. Brother Gregor hadn't been so lucky, as they had found his bullet-shredded body dumped in the tunnel.

Bolan strode into the lobby. It was a drab affair inside, poorly lit, with a ceiling fan slapping at hot air. Bullet holes were left in the walls and smattering of furniture, as if the scars of civil war were trophies to be displayed. As luck would have it, Bolan found no one loitering in the lobby. He made a beeline for the desk clerk, who was hunched over a magazine. The Yemeni was a front man for the Russian operation, and Bolan wasn't about to let the old guy off the hook for bad judgment. The clerk saw the big American coming his way and dropped the magazine. His eyes widened with fear, some primal instinct warning him the stranger wasn't there to book a room for the night.

Bolan grabbed the clerk by his shirtfront, hammering a right cross off the guy's jaw, lights out. He took the plastic cuffs, slapped them on the guy's wrists, then took the duct tape he had brought especially for this encounter. He peeled off a strip, pasted it over the clerk's mouth then dragged him into a back room.

Bolan had to work quickly. The CIA contact had laid out his evac, a stairway that ran from the fourth floor to a back alley. Once he was clear of the hotel premises, the soldier was to radio his man in Yemen for a rendezvous two blocks north. If it turned ugly on the drive out of the city—meaning Yemeni authorities showed up—well, Bolan would deal with it then, quick and lethal.

First things first.

Bolan unleathered the Beretta and gave the lobby a quick search, clear on his end. He began climbing the stairs.

PAVLOVKA AND HIS three-man hit team went to work as soon as they entered the prince's room. They were all gathered, staring his way. The prince and Hezbollah flunkies in one corner, the Somali warlord and his four-man entourage seated in another corner, everyone's moneybags within easy reach. Pavlovka could almost smell the greed in the stifling heat.

It was the six Pakistanis, though, who took Pavlovka's full and lethal attention. Under his earlier orders, every man in the bidding war had been relieved of weapons.

So the hit was easy, swift and bloody, with minimum

resistance, but maximum outrage and horror. Pavlovka saw mouths gaping, eyes bulging, screams or curses about to rip the air when he started squeezing the Makarov's trigger over and over. The Pakistanis were grouped tight, lined up against the wall beside the window. Easy pickings.

Deadweight crunched to the floor, crimson pools spreading from six convulsing bodies. It was a clean sweep, but the show had only just begun.

General Akeem Assal was leaping to his feet, his initial shock and horror giving way to outrage. "What is this? You're going to murder us all and take our money! We had a deal! You bastards..."

The Russians slapped fresh clips into their pistols, cocked and locked. Pavlovka gave the Somali warlord a fleeting moment of contemptuous consideration. Before him stood a hypocritical worm. A man who had plundered and raped the economy of his country, sold weapons and drugs, seized all financial and food aid from the United States and allies, with the help, of course, of many of his cronies in Mogadishu. A man exiled in disgrace when international law enforcement agencies closed in, who had bought his way out of Somalia and ingratiated himself with the junkie prince. A man pumped on dreams of returning to his homeland to seize the country and surrounding nations by using nuclear blackmail.

The Russians burned through their clips, dropping the Somalis in a tangled heap in a matter of seconds.

Pavlovka laid a cold smile on the prince and cronies, all of them frozen in terror. "Relax, prince, it seems your price, though not quite right, has won you the honors for first bid."

Suddenly, when the whole room erupted in a blinding white light. Pavlovka found his senses shattered. It was all he could do to stay standing, trying to get it together as his brain felt cleaved in half.

A moment later, Igor Pavlovka discovered pain was the last and least of his problems in Yemen, or on earth for that matter.

THERE WAS SOMETHING to be said, the Executioner thought, about timing being everything in life, some cosmic justice, divine intervention even stepping in and lending the good fight a helping hand.

The soldier had topped the stairs to the targeted floor, was moving down the hallway, about to do a room-to-room sweep when he discovered the savages were ahead, and eating one another alive.

It helped Bolan cover his surge and get down to business. He opted for the compact submachine gun, intent on using the flash-stun grenade to lead the charge. He heard a voice of anger raised, followed up by the familiar chugging of sound-suppressed pistols, then more deadweight thudding. With an underhanded pitch, hearing someone naming and addressing the Saudi prince, Bolan lobbed the flash-stun through the doorway. He covered his eyes, rode out the thunderclap and the blinding strobe of white light.

He went in hard, Ingram MAC-10 leading the way, spared no one.

The Executioner stood, tall and grim in the doorway, raking the MAC-10 flank to flank, catching them in the back. Smoke and dust boiling before him, the soldier tracked on with the SMG. They spun, screamed and pitched all over the place, blood taking to the smoky air.

As the smoke thinned the warrior took in the carnage. The Somali warlord and flunkies, and six bodies of undetermined nationality stacked up against the base of the west wall. Then the Saudi prince and Hezbollah pals, stretched out, leaking gore, strewed directly before the Executioner.

No Vlad Drakovich.

With the ringing in his ears diminishing, Bolan tuned in to any sounds of encroachment from the hall or the street. Nothing. It was time to fly.

The Executioner turned and left the slaughterhouse, the bidding war over, a done deal.

18

The air-and-ground strike on the reprocessing plant and hardsite was slated to go down just before dawn. According to his chronometer and based on word from Stony Man Farm the first light of day would break over the jagged ridges of the hills in less than fifty minutes.

The soldier hadn't expected to find any of the enemy troops nodding off or shuffling through the motions of sentry duty. Bolan wasn't disappointed by his mental pregauging when he finally reached his long-range observation point on the edge of a hill, roughly five hundred meters due west of the compound. There was a nuclear prize or more at the end of line for the opposition, after all, and nobody was about to sleep that night.

They looked agitated, indeed, smelling trouble closing in maybe, if he read the faces that were framed in the scope of his high-powered infrared binoculars right. Down on the runway, armed shadows were bustling around the scattered klieg lights. Still more AK-47-toting silhouettes filtered in and out of the soft white glow where the mouth of the tunnel led to the underground complex, containing the light-water reactor and the radioactive waste that had clearly shown up on satellite imagery. And, of course, whatever other hellish devices of mass destruction were kept down there.

The big prize, human or otherwise, was yet to be seized, but the Executioner had found his man on-site. He already knew that Vlad Drakovich, though, was at the complex. A United States AWACS, on loan to Bolan and company from the U.S. military base in Riyadh, had tracked the massive Antonov transport on radar when it had crossed Oman airspace before flying west into Yemen, a little more than three hours ago. Six F-15s had made visual sighting of the Antonov jet, but as ordered by the U.S. commander of operations in the area via Brognola, they dropped off. The F-15s were on standing orders to recon the skies of Yemen, with possible fire support for Grimaldi and crew thrown into the picture once the AC-130 gunship made its rude appearance there. There was a Yemeni military base fifty klicks or so west of the hardsite, complete with ten grounded MiGs and three Mi-24 Hind gunships. If the enemy was in radio contact with the base and MiGs and gunships were scrambled when the action went down, all Yemeni fighting aircraft were ordered to be engaged and blown out of the sky by the marauding F-15s.

Bolan wasn't looking for some protracted engagement nor did he want to create an ugly international incident that would further fan the flames of hostility and aggression in the Middle East. Just the same, he wanted all bases covered, and he would do whatever it took to crush the enemy here, make sure his people went home standing, nuclear packages in tow. It was fourth and goal for the visiting team in Yemen, and the clock was ticking down.

Bolan lowered the field glasses, pulled back from the ridge. On his way up the hill he had already searched the area for sentries, but found no armed shadows standing watch. It stood to reason all available hands were down there, making good on the delivery and guarding the store within arms' reach.

It had been a hard and anxious drive, lights out, followed by an advance on foot up the hill just to get to this stage.

After clearing the city limits of Aden with his CIA escort, Bolan had switched off to a waiting Humvee, as pre-arranged. In a secret compartment in the bed of the Humvee, the CIA contact had come through with more items Bolan requested. A passing of intel between the soldier and the CIA man in Yemen, and the soldier had rolled on solo, M-16/M-203 combo leaning against the passenger seat the whole way. He had frag, incendiary and flash-stun grenades for the M-203, along with spare clips for the assault rifle.

Aden seemed a distant memory now, but he had left behind quite the mess for someone to sort through.

What would happen to all the money he had left scattered in the hotel's slaughter bed was anybody's guess. There might be a mad scramble, with Yemen authorities and the CIA each claiming ownership of all that cash. Not his problem.

Brognola and Stony Man Farm had gone the extra mile, ironing out logistics, shoring up details, inserting the blacksuit team. Using the blacksuits from the Farm on this strike was an unusual situation, bucking normal Farm protocol. Ordinarily Bolan should have gone in with Able Team and Phoenix Force, but the other Stony Man warriors were engaged in other missions right then and couldn't be pulled off. So be it. It might shave the security detail at the Farm to a skeleton crew, but Brognola knew how grim Bolan's mission was. More than a little help from friends and the home team, indeed, and the Executioner intended to make the efforts of all concerned pay off. His force had been briefed, mission parameters defined, fire teams assigned by number and individual combatants given letter designation. When the heat was on, a white star on the shoulder of each blacksuit would separate friendlies from hostiles. Bolan had already fixed the adhesive white star on his shoulder.

Bolan hadn't used a road map or the word of a dead former KGB assassin to get him to the hardsite, either. Secured around his forearm was an instrument the size of a cell phone. He was linked to NavStar, or a global positioning satellite. The GPS had beamed a signal to a B-1 bomber over the Arabian Sea where it was then received by the soldier. It had steered him down the paved Aden-al Mukalla road, deep into the province of Abyan, and then managed to get him straight to the enemy's doorstep after running a winding series of dirt stretches off the main course. In contact with Stony Man Farm via his secure radio line, Bolan was guided by Kurtzman away from all checkpoints and roadblocks using satellite imagery.

Bolan had very little idea of what they might actually find below ground, much less hard intel on enemy numbers, which told him the stink of corruption reached far and wide. Silence had proved golden for the enemy in this case, a silence about to be shattered.

Bolan made another surveillance of the compound. He took a rough head count, figured maybe sixty or so guns, including Drakovich and his Mafia killers. There was a long and low-lying stone structure north of the runway. That would be the barracks that housed troops and workers, both laborers and technicians. Panning on, Bolan looked at the water tower, three huge fuel drums at the south edge of open terrain that spread away from the mountain range. There was a motor pool in that direction, with a mix of two dozen or so Jeeps and transport trucks.

Pretty basic setup, all in all. Other than the gunmen satellite imagery had picked up, it could, on the surface, pass for a small oil field. There wasn't even an antiaircraft battery on hand, and that was a definite plus for Grimaldi and crew. Of course, Bolan couldn't discount the fact there might be RPG-7 rocket launchers lying around, even a Stinger or two, which could knock out his fire support. He had no choice but to take it as it showed.

Another twenty minutes passed, then Bolan heard his headset crackle. Grimaldi came through the comm-link, loud and clear. "Wolf Runner to Steel Talon, come in."

Bolan went on-line. "Steel Talon here. I'm in position. I take it you have an ETA for me."

"We're making our approach now. Five minutes and counting. I'm reading your signal on my screen, I'm nearly on top of you. I'll make the drop where we agreed. What's the situation on your end?"

"We're good to go. Once you make the drop, see that your first strafing run's a beauty. It's open season. Copy that, Wolf Runner."

"Roger that, Steel Talon. All systems go on this end. See you when the smoke clears."

Grimaldi signed off, and Bolan picked up his M-16. He searched the skies behind him, began making his move down the south side of the hill for the drop zone. On the way, he heard the first distant rumble of thunder, rolling toward him from the northwest.

It was show time.

VLAD DRAKOVICH could barely contain his rage. It had been two hours or so since he left the airplane. Every last one of his soldiers were around him, all of them armed to the teeth, with everyone burning inside to seal the deal. And he was finding he liked Yemen even less than Pakistan.

First he was caked in the dried blood of his brother, his nose full of the reminder of Gregor's death, his clothes also coated by the slime of sewage and chemicals that had slicked him on his way out of the tunnel back in Karachi. The stink alone made him want to puke, at best, and reminded him of another failure, at worst. Second, he was being jerked around and stalled by a Yemeni Major Jabal al-Narib, who was supposedly their man in Yemen. Narib, the impertinent bastard, had ordered the Russians to remain outside the reprocessing plant, near the runway. The merchandise was down there, he was informed by Narib, but there were some problems, matters to discuss. What problems? What matters? Without explaining, Narib had left him standing with his troops while he marched back into the tunnel.

That was a good hour ago. What the hell was going on?

The only plus was that Pavlovka had had half of the Saudi's money delivered as promised. Three duffel bags, bulging with rubber-banded stacks of American hundred-dollar bills, lay at Drakovich's feet. He wasn't about to let the money out of his sight. While he waited for Narib's return, he chewed on his nerves, sucked on rage, fighting down the urge to just pull the Uzi SMG off his shoulder and make the Yemeni dance to his tune. Which was round up the merchandise, load it on the Antonov jet so Drakovich could roll out at the first inkling of any further delays or problems. And where was Pavlovka and their bidding parties anyway? No word from Aden, no one able to reach Pavlovka, just a chilling dead silence at Pavlovka's end.

Drakovich felt the eyes of his men all over him, silently urging him to do something, anything. He searched the vast darkness of the plain stretching away to the south. Something was wrong, he could feel it in the darkness, the silence out there. It was the same sort of icy feeling he'd experienced in Pakistan, Russia and America. Visions of their mystery American shooters wanted to burn through his mind but he steeled himself, determined to settle up here, one way or another. He couldn't lose face or resolve, not in front of his men at this critical juncture. Besides, there was no way his nemesis could have tracked him to Yemen.

"I don't like this delay, Comrade. I see Pakistan all over again."

Drakovich turned, looked at Dtechka and nodded. "Pass the word on to the others," he said in Russian. "If they see me go for my gun they are to back my play. If the major wants to go for broke, you are to kill him and his Yemeni soldiers."

It was something he would never have thought he would tell himself since the will had fallen into his hands. But things had changed, and not even his father could have foreseen all the disasters the elder son had faced. All of a sudden he was beginning to doubt everything about this project his father and Smolenskov had created. It was falling apart at every turn, had been since Brighton Beach. His love for and belief in his father and loyalty to his own word had cemented his stubborn refusal to see any other course of action. But now, with his brother dead, the SS-20 taken out of their possession, sensing trouble ahead with the Yemenis... Well, at least he had the money, or some money. Plus the merchandise was within reach. He could take it by force, fly on to Moscow. There, regroup, rebuild his organization. Perhaps use all the other business endeavors of his inherited kingdom to launch another nuclear-smuggling operation someday, but a deal that went straight with missiles stolen right out of depots or silos, not this business of reprocessing radioactive waste, using mules, cutouts, fanatics, whatever.

Or was he rationalizing his own fear and doubt, justifying some urge to bail out of his father's wishes simply because he was still alive, with money to burn and an empire to salvage?

"We will take the merchandise at gunpoint and fly out of this godforsaken hellhole." He snapped to attention as he spotted the Yemeni major approaching.

"Well?" Drakovich barked.

"We need to discuss a most serious matter."

The Yemeni paused, flanked by two of his cronies in buff-colored uniforms and holding AK-47s.

"Goddammit, what?"

The major flinched, scowled at the anger flung his way, but forged on. "Certain promises were made to me long ago by your father when this project was undertaken. And at great risk to myself, I may add. Some of the payoffs were necessary for silencing of loose tongues on my part. Well, I was personally guaranteed two of the nuclear shells once production was completed. I'm pleased to report production has been achieved."

There it was, the bottom line. Enough games, dancing around. He was sick of other people's greed and bullshit.

Vlad Drakovich was feeling his blood boil with rage. He knew where this was headed. His heart was pumping with murder and his hand slid for the Uzi when something that sounded like distant thunder broke through the ringing, brought on by fury and rising blood pressure, in his ears.

Then he saw the look of fear all around him, as all eyes stared past him. He was turning, trying to make out the sound, make sense of their show of anxiety and confusion, when he thought he saw figures falling from the sky to the southwest, shapes that were hanging from parachutes. Shadows that were already hitting the earth as the realization of what was happening took shape in his mind.

Then the rolling thunder found its point of origin in his gaze. The dark behemoth bulk in the air dipped its wing beyond the hills to the west, straightened out and began a nose-first descent for the runway.

No, scratch that, it was a strafing run, he suspected.

Vlad Drakovich heard the cursing and shouting and general pandemonium breaking out around him. The Yemenis even began firing at the giant bird with AK-47s, as if they could bring it down with a few bullets to the fuselage. The stupid bastards.

The Boss almost laughed out loud, but couldn't, the laughter choking in his throat. It was time to act—hell, no, it was time to run. Primal instinct and a burning desire to save himself and somehow rebuild the kingdom he had inherited seized Vlad Drakovich.

A moment later what he already feared would happen became yet another harsh reality.

The sky seemed to erupt above Vlad Drakovich, all fire, fury and rolling thunder. It sounded like some horrible prelude to his personal apocalypse.

19

It was a vision of hell on earth.

The blacksuits were hitting the ground at the end of their six-hundred-foot combat jump, chutes off, dropping the packs containing the biochem-nuke decontamination suits, to be left behind until the underground complex was taken down and secured.

Bolan was moving out from the drop zone, leading his own designated team, all hands cocked and locked on their M-16s, breeches of M-203s loaded with 40 mm shells, when he was damn near blinded by the fireworks pounding the hardsite. It was a vicious assault on his senses. It jarred Bolan to the bone, the ground shaking underfoot, the air superheated and reaching out with scorching winds and bullish concussive force, even at five hundred meters. The soldier kept running, full speed. Not even the gas mask and small satchel of grenades and tear gas canisters handed over by a blacksuit at the drop zone could slow him at this point.

The Executioner was familiar with the firepower of Spectre. He knew the AC-130 war bird was a decimator of small armies and could turn a dozen or so tanks into flaming scrap in about the time it takes to burn through an M-16's clip.

The eye of the storm passed right over what Bolan

figured was the bulk of enemy numbers. Dead ahead, it was keep-it-simple on its most basic level. No smart bombs, no Tomahawks and cruise missiles, locked on to target from a thousand miles out. Here, in the belly of the beast, it was pour it on at near point-blank range.

Bolan had seen Spectre in action before, and this time out the war bird once again proved itself up to a task of total and utter annihilation of man, machine and anything else unfortunate enough to be caught in its talons.

On the run, the Executioner couldn't help but tip his hat to the way Grimaldi and crew paved their run to the killing field. The black-camouflaged fixed-wing gunship was a predatory monster bird, to say the least. Four 20 mm cannons, same number of 7.62 mm miniguns on the nose end. Add to the wings of this beast a couple of Vulcan 20 mm cannons, one Bofors gun along with a mounted 105 mm howitzer in the open doorway. With all of this firepower electronically controlled by the tried-and-true hands of Grimaldi and company. The enemy could watch it roll up before their eyes in a blinding flash of fire and deafening thunderclaps.

Which was exactly what happened.

The Antonov went first, obliterated to hunks of flaming metal that winged out for a hundred meters or more in all directions. Its fuel was ignited by the Spectre hammering, and a shrieking wave of fire reached out, dropped over several unfortunates left standing along the runway, turning them into human fireballs. So much for any enemy evac, by air at least. Cannons pounded on, relentless peals of death trumpeting the road to hell, miniguns flaming away, chewing up flesh and turning men into crimson Swiss cheese as the monster sailed over the compound. The water tower went next, with the fuel depot lost in mushrooming balls of fire in a following heartbeat. Half of the motor pool then absorbed a terrible raking of cannon fire, vehicles flung in all directions.

There were so many explosions in a few heartbeats, so much debris flying everywhere and figures sailing around on all points of the compass it was hard to assess how much damage Spectre had wreaked.

The war bird gave the mouth of the tunnel a quick spray of minigun fire, while another cannon burst uprooted the barracks as it flew past, then it nosed up and soared over the mountain range.

Death from above had done its part.

It was time for Bolan and the blacksuits to get busy.

Four five-man teams—with Bolan's Team X the odd one out with six guns—had to run at least two hundred meters before they were within range with the M-16s. It would give any wounded survivors looking either to fight back or to make a run for freedom time to get it in gear.

The Executioner was on the lookout for live ones.

Spectre was rumbling off to the east, the port wing dipping as Grimaldi began to swing the war bird around. Grimaldi and crew would come back, but this time only to provide selective cover-fire support.

As his M-16 was fanning the flames ahead for targets, Bolan had difficulty at first finding anything left alive. He knew they were beyond the inferno, scrambling somewhere to break out of the paths of all the raining slabs of wreckage. Armed shadows were, indeed, already scrambling in the Executioner's death sights.

It was run and gun from there on. Nothing tricky,

nothing fancy. Victory would be decided by nothing less than old-fashioned guts and nerve, and the will to kill. Nothing more, nothing less.

Bolan's team was the spearhead, the other fire teams spread out on his flanks. Each charging team maintained a dozen-meter-or-so gap from the other, not giving the enemy a chance to mow them down in twos or threes or worse with sustained fire.

Enemy traffic showed beyond the inferno, clear and defined now. They were bumping, twisting and careening all over the place. Some of them were scattering like hell, no doubt bloodied senseless. Return fire sought out the blacksuited chargers, but Bolan and company rocked the compound with a salvo of 40 mm grenades, shredding apart the human traffic. A pocket of resistance erupted from the heaped rubble of the barracks. Maybe ten muzzle-flashes stabbed the gloom that way. The soldier patched through to Grimaldi, informed him of the enemy pocket. The pilot copied Bolan, had the friendly positions marked on his infrared tracking screen. Thanks to their homing beacons they would show up, green, as opposed to red for the enemy on Grimaldi's console.

Spectre thundered over the inferno, giving the friendlies a wide berth before a combined storm of cannon and minigun fire decimated the pocket in question.

Hungry flames reached out for Bolan as he skirted past a graveyard of wreckage, lakes of fire and strewed corpses. There were wounded, moaning and crawling around, some rising on bloodied limbs. Bolan held back on the trigger of his assault rifle, cutting them down if they reached for a weapon or tried to stand. On the fly the Executioner mowed down a trio of stragglers while his troops added to the slaughter. He checked his flanks. They were all on one frequency, all tied in likewise to Spectre.

Bolan asked for a casualty report, found his team intact and moving ahead. Then, seeing about a dozen or so figures surging out of the tunnel's mouth, the Executioner gave his ground troops the order to be ready with phase Blinding Light. Digging into his satchel, he hauled out and loaded up the breech of his M-203 with a flash-stun grenade. They were less than two hundred meters from the tunnel.

Bolan dropped to one knee and gave the order to commence firing. In sync with his people, he squeezed the M-203's trigger. Flash-stun grenades were everywhere, zigzagging on tails of smoke and flame. Bolan hit the ground, closed his eyes as a tremendous thunderclap and supernova of white light filled the mouth of the tunnel, and beyond. Up and running, the soldier gave the killing field a hard search. Autofire chattered ahead, bullets gouging up divots of turf at his feet. He was tracking two shadows who held their ground near the flaming Antonov, when Team Z on his right flank took care of that particular problem.

"Steel Talon, I've got a lone runner heading for the motor pool. He's armed, and he's carrying a couple of large duffel bags. I can't make a visual but my gut's telling me it's Drakovich."

It made twisted sense, at least from the Russian's perspective. This was a wrap, a done deal, and there was nothing left here for the man who would be king to take home from Yemen.

Ahead, Bolan saw several figures coughing and stumbling from the smoking maw of the tunnel. They held weapons, and they were firing blind. They lasted all of three seconds as the enemy got an especially gruesome twenty-one-gun salute from the black-clad marauders.

Bolan scanned the battlefield. Nothing stirred, not even a groan sounded. He spoke into his throat mike, giving the order for all teams to proceed ahead, throw flash-stun grenades into the tunnel, then use tear gas.

Bolan told the leader of Team W, "I've got a situation I need to see taken care of, up close and personal. I'm peeling off. I figure you've got nothing left but token resistance below. When it's secured below, Team X and Z will fall back, retrieve the HAZMAT suits and go down there. I want whatever they've got in terms of missiles, shells or whatever loaded up on Spectre. Copy that."

"Roger that."

Bolan was moving out, fully confident his people could take it from there. "Wolf Runner, come in," Bolan said, forced to shout above the roar of fire in his ears. The Executioner was heading in the direction of the lake of fire engulfing at least half of the motor pool. Firelight outlined the solitary figure. As he closed and the figure turned his way, Bolan made out the face of the man he had chased across four countries. Even at a distance, Bolan would have sworn the man who would be king made eye contact with him.

Vlad Drakovich piled into a Jeep containing the duffel bags Bolan was sure were stuffed with loot. Naturally one or two strafings from Spectre wouldn't have knocked out everything in the motor pool, not when they were concentrating primarily on moving targets along the compound proper. Bolan set his sights on a group of Jeeps, intact on the periphery of the firestorm.

"Wolf Runner here, Steel Talon. Awaiting further orders."

"I want you down here and I want those payloads loaded up. Then get the hell out of here."

"And if we've got prisoners, or wounded?"

Bolan knew what Grimaldi was asking. He gave it a moment's consideration, just the same. But cold-blooded killing of unarmed opposition or civilians, no matter how dirty or involved they were in this operation, didn't sit well with Bolan.

"If that happens, tie them up and leave them. I want you airborne again, ASAP, either way. Stay in the air and wait to hear from me."

"Affirmative. I've got all radio frequencies, military and police, monitored. So far there's nothing but dead air on all local channels. I don't know if that will hold up. There's a village not far to the east and they're sure to hear this racket by now."

"I understand. I'll try to make it quick. I'll be in touch. Over and out."

The Jeep Drakovich commandeered was bulling through some wreckage, sluicing out from the inferno, then whipping ahead. It seemed to take an agonizing eternity but the soldier finally reached the few vehicles intact. He found the keys in the ignition of a Jeep, hopped in and fired up the vehicle.

THE FIRST LIGHT of a new day was breaking over terraced hills beyond the stone huts of the small village when the Executioner closed on the Jeep. He was less than two hundred meters away now, having followed the spool of dust over hard and uneven ground. Drakovich knew by now he was tagged.

Bolan already had a full sit-rep from Grimaldi's end, and the report was some measure of comfort. The reprocessing plant was a primitive, seat-of-the-pants operation. No silos, but a lot of radioactive waste dumped in lead containers below ground. It was a hot zone down there, according to Grimaldi's Geiger counter. Four 155 shells and two suitcases had been hauled up a freight elevator, dollied up Spectre's ramp. The suitcases were rough copies of the kind of nuclear backpacks developed by the U.S. Special Forces. The enemy below, as Bolan suspected, had offered a token resistance, but were cut down by the blacksuits while they reeled around in tear gas clouds. There were no survivors on the compound, above or below ground. Apparently whatever technicians and physicists were on hand had opted to swallow cyanide.

Grimaldi was already airborne with the payload.

It was all Bolan cared to know right then.

Ahead, closing the gap to his enemy, the soldier saw Drakovich turn the Jeep around the corner of a row of huts. Bolan barreled his vehicle down the dirt street where a goat and several chickens scattered out of his path. In this part of Yemen, he could be sure the male populace was armed. He hoped they didn't get over-agitated or trigger-happy at this point. His fight wasn't with them.

He rounded the corner, spotted the Jeep sitting in a cloud of steam at the end of the street. Combat senses on full alert, a full clip in his M-16, Bolan piled out. He gave his surroundings a hard search. Shadows stayed put in doorways. He didn't find any weapons tracking him at the moment.

Suddenly autofire rang out from inside a hut at the end of the street. He saw the steam rising from the hood of Drakovich's Jeep and knew the Don had either blown a gasket, or Spectre had nailed the engine during its initial strafe, leaving Drakovich with a vehicle that could only get him this far.

Bolan moved down the street. He had a grim notion of what had happened inside that hut. Drakovich had snapped, was demanding a vehicle, most likely. Where he thought he could go was a moot point.

A moment later the man's insanity was confirmed as Drakovich emerged from the doorway with a hostage.

"Get back, you bastard!"

Bolan slowed his pace, M-16 at port arms. He gave the small boy clutched in Drakovich's arm a look, searching for an opening to nail his enemy. The Mob boss was jockeying for position on Bolan, straining to lug the boy along as a shield. With the duffel bags hooked over the arm where an Uzi was clutched at the end, Drakovich was having trouble getting his aim right.

The Executioner switched the selector mode to one-shot. Drakovich stumbled, screaming curses. By now, Bolan had a crowd of spectators. He sensed the villagers knew the score here, could clearly read the madness in the eyes of Drakovich and knew there was only one way to deal with this savage.

Bolan fired a single 5.56 mm round, drilling Drakovich in the upper chest. On a spurt of blood, Drakovich toppled backward, hitting the ground with a grunt and a puff of dust. The boy ran.

"You bastard!" Drakovich screamed. "Listen, listen to me! I've got money. I can split this with you!"

It was a last-ditch gasp. Closing on the Russian and flicking the selector switch back to full-auto, Bolan told the man whose reign as Don was about to prove short and bitter, "No sale."

"Why?"

Drakovich struggled to stand, clutching the duffel bags, swinging his Uzi around.

"You wouldn't understand," Bolan simply said, then cut loose, the M-16 chattering out a long sweeping burst, side to side, toe to head. The soldier's lead storm blasted open the duffel bags, flinging their contents in Drakovich's face. The line of 5.56 mm lead finished with a couple of rounds to Drakovich's chest.

The Executioner gave the onlookers a search for any threat. None showed. In the distance, he caught the faint and familiar rumble.

Bolan turned and walked toward his Jeep. He left Drakovich where he lay, stretched out beside the only thing that had mattered to him.

James Axler

OUTLANDERS™

WREATH OF FIRE

Ambika, an amazon female, has been gathering groups of
Outlanders in the Western Isles in an attempt to overthrow
the Barons. But are her motives just a ploy to satisfy her
own ambition?

GOUT12